The Bacardi Girls

Spoiled, Bad & Bougie

A novel by Lady Lissa

Connect with me!

Facebook:
https://www.facebook.com/AuthoressLadyLissa

Twitter: https://twitter.com/LadyLissa832

Instagram: lady_lissa832

TikTok: TheRealLady_Lissa

Email: ladylissa832@gmail.com

Prologue

Jerrika Bacardi

Man, this shit was really starting to piss me off. We had been putting up with the same old shit since we were teenagers. That was the main reason me and my sisters wanted to leave this area and apartment when we were old enough to go to college. My first choice for college was Texas Southern University, but Saderia and Zaria said that wasn't far enough.

"I've always wanted to go to Atlanta cuz that's where black stars are born!" Saderia said.

"Shit, I wouldn't mind going there!" Zaria cheered.

"That's so far," I said. "We don't have any money, so how are we gonna get there?"

At the time, Saderia was a junior, Zaria was a sophomore, and I was in middle school. These were just conversations we liked to have concerning our future. We grew up in a roach infested apartment in the projects, so we knew in order for us to have a better life, we had to get away from here.

I was all for leaving the apartment, but I didn't know we were thinking about going all the way to Atlanta. We all agreed to get jobs and save money to help us get to the Atlanta area.

Of course, at the time, I was too young to work, but once I made fifteen, I got a worker's permit and a job at Baskin Robbins. By that time, my sisters had both left home, so it was just me and mom.

Now, here we were, years later, back in Houston visiting our mom because school was starting next week. We had been here for nine days and was heading back to school Wednesday because I had stuff to do. But of course, our mom had other plans.

The entire time we had been visiting, she had been entertaining strange men under the same roof where we slept. The tiny apartment had only two bedrooms and one bathroom, so my sisters and I had been sharing a room since we were kids. Of course, it was a little more uncomfortable now that we were in our twenties.

So, I was laying in bed trying to drown out the noises I could clearly hear coming from our mama's bedroom next door. The walls were thin like paper so I could hear every moan, kiss, slap on the ass, and the bed creaking too. Just disgusting.

My sisters weren't home at the time, at least I didn't think they were since they weren't in the room. I took a pillow and pulled it over my head to try and drown out the noise, but that didn't work. I thought our mom was very selfish for inviting dudes to come here when she knew we were here. It was like she didn't give a shit how we felt, if it woke us up, if we could hear her... nothing. And this was literally the fourth time this week that her and some dude woke me up out of my sleep.

I watched the movie, *Baby Boy*, so I knew mama had to have a life too, but damn! All I wanted was a little respect. R-E-S-P-E-C-T! Ain't that what Ms. Aretha Franklin said we all deserved? Why couldn't she have gone to a motel with that nigga?

I mean, he wasn't her nigga! Why did she always have to bring that shit here when she knew we were trying to sleep? Unlike her, I had stuff to do tomorrow, so I needed my beauty sleep.

The last thing I wanted to hear was my mom getting her coochie busted wide open at one o'clock in the. Just ugh!

All I wanted was to get some sleep, but how could I when I knew what she was doing in the room next door to me.

"Man, do y'all hear this shit?" I asked as I sat up in bed frustrated.

Of course, I was talking to myself because neither one of those heifers were in their bed. I was so sick of this shit and was about to go check my mom's ass when I heard a loud thud. It sounded like somebody had fell hard on the floor. I listened carefully to see what else I'd hear and when I realized what was really going on, I sprang into action.

I jumped out of bed when I heard my mom moaning and crying. I heard loud slaps and the man hollering at her. It didn't take long for me figure out that she was getting her ass whooped. The first thing I did was reach into my purse and pull out my taser. Being single on campus, I had to protect myself, so I carried that taser everywhere.

As quickly opened my bedroom door and it creaked a little. As I made my way to my mom's room, I heard what sounded like the dude punching her. I wasted no time rushing into my mom's bedroom. I swung the door open and sure enough, there was a strange man standing over her beating the dog shit out of her.

He was swinging on her like she was a grown ass man. The nigga was butt naked, so I came up behind him and hit him dead in his hairy ass with the volts of the taser. His hands immediately flew up in the air as I kept the shock going. I was going to keep shocking his ass until he was no longer a threat to my mom. His body finally collapsed on the floor, shaking like a fish out of water while he moaned and whined in pain. My sisters appeared out of nowhere and busted into the bedroom. I screamed for them to call 9-1-1.

I could not believe this shit was even happening right now. Over the course of the past week, we had several arguments with our mom about bringing strange men to the apartment. She got mad and blew up at us... talking about this was her house and she could do what she wanted. She even went as far as telling us if we didn't like it, we could leave.

That was crazy for her to tell us that after we came all the way here to visit her. We didn't have to come here. We could have stayed in Atlanta for all this shit. We were scheduled to leave in two days because me and Zaria started school the following Monday. Instead of enjoying her time with us, our mom was doing what she did when we weren't here... drugs and men.

But what if that man had torn into her tonight and I wouldn't have been here? That man could have and probably would have killed her!

As Saderia, my oldest sister, and I tended to our mom, I heard Zaria on the phone with the 9-1-1 operator. She was frantically trying to explain what happened, but was so nervous, even I couldn't comprehend what she was trying to say. I knew if I couldn't understand, the operator couldn't either.

"Zaria please calm down and just tell her to send a damn ambulance and the police to arrest this muthafucka!" I stated as I kicked him as hard as I could.

I went around him to the one bathroom we all shared down the hall. I filled a bucket with water and grabbed a washcloth.

"Mom, you alright?" Saderia asked.

"Of course, she's not alright!" I barked.

"Well, I know she's not totally alright! I'm just wondering if she's alive!" Saderia retorted. "Mom! Mom!" Our mom didn't respond, which worried both of us.

"Oh my God! Is she dead?" Zaria frantically screamed.

"I don't think so! Her chest is still moving," Saderia responded. "She's probably just knocked the hell out! Look at her damn face!"

Our mom's face had been pummeled to the point where we couldn't even recognize her. "The ambulance is on the way!" Zaria informed us.

I took the towel from the bucket and said, "You hear that mom. The ambulance is coming!"

Her eyes finally fluttered open as I started to wipe some of the blood from her face. She groaned in pain as she tried to move her swollen lips to say something.

"Don't talk!" Saderia instructed.

"No! No! NO!" she mumbled weakly.

"Mom chill! The cops and ambulance are on the way!" I said as I continued to try and clean her face. "Mom we told you to stop inviting these losers over here!"

"Yea mom! What do you think would have happened to you if we wouldn't have been here?"

Saderia asked angrily. "You could have been killed by this asshole!"

Fifteen minutes had passed before we finally heard the sirens in the near distance. Zaria bolted from the room, probably to let the paramedics in. Saderia stood up and grabbed mom's robe off the hook inside her closet. The man moved slightly so I grabbed my taser and shot him with the volts once again. His body shook savagely until Saderia told me to stop.

"STOP JERRIKA!! You're gonna kill him!" she yelled.

"Good! He almost killed mom! So, I don't give a fuck what happens to him!"

Saderia covered mom's nude body with the robe as Zaria rushed in with the police. "There he is!" she said as she pointed to the strange man lying on the floor.

"What happened to him?" the officer asked.

"I shocked him with my taser when I caught him beating the hell out of my mom!" I explained.

"Sir! SIR!" the officer called as he slapped his face on both sides.

It took several minutes, but the man finally opened his eyes. "Wh-wh-what happened?" he asked as he looked around with a look of confusion on his face.

"We need to take you down to the station," the officer said as he and the other officer lifted the naked man off the floor.

"Take me in! What for?" he asked in a slurred tone.

"Assault!" the cop said.

"Assault! But she assaulted me!" he argued.

"After you almost beat our mom to death, you asshole!" I yelled. "You are so lucky the police are here because if they weren't, I'd zap your ass again!"

"See! She just threatened me!" the man fussed.

"Sir, I need you to grab your clothes and put them on," the officer instructed in a stern tone as he looked the guy in the face.

"Oh my fucking God! So, you are really arresting me! After that little bitch tased my ass!" he asked angrily.

"That's what I said. Now, you can either put your clothes on, or we can run down to the station just the way you are," the officer warned with an attitude.

"I can't believe I'm getting arrested! You should be arresting that prostitute!" he fussed.

"Prostitute!" Saderia shrieked. "Our mom isn't a prostitute!"

"When you're a prostitute, you get paid," Zaria said as she looked around the room. "Does anyone see any money anywhere? Cuz I sure don't!" Zaria stated with an attitude. "Did you pay her any money before you decided to whoop her ass?"

"Well, no, but..."

"Come on sir," the officers said as they dragged the guy out in cuffs.

All the way out the door, I could hear the man arguing because he was being arrested.

"Where the hell are the medics?" I asked.

"We had to get the suspect out of here and secure the scene before we allow the medics in," the officer explained in a kind voice. At least he didn't appear to be judging us, which I was grateful for.

Once the officers had dragged his ass out, the medics rushed in to help our mother. They loaded her on the stretcher and headed with her to the ambulance. Me and my sisters quickly got dressed and headed to the hospital.

This was crazy! If our mom didn't change the way she lived, the next time she brought a dude home would probably be her last!

Thank God we were here!

Chapter one

Jerrika

That was not how I expected my night to end. Earlier, I was walking around singing because I couldn't wait until Wednesday. Me and my sisters were heading back to Atlanta and the life we knew. The only reason we came here in the first place was because we were starting school soon and wanted to check on our mom. Even though we had only been here for a week, I was ready to go.

The whole time we were here, mom spent it entertaining men. It was almost like we weren't even here. Hearing that man call her a prostitute had me wondering if she was really charging for her cookies. The last thing I wanted to think about was her selling coochie for a fix.

Our mom had always struggled with an addiction to drugs. It started years ago when she had an accident at work and hurt her back. It started with prescription drugs, but eventually, she the doctor stopped prescribing them because she felt like our mom was becoming addicted, and she was right.

But by then, it was too late. It was like she went from Lortab to heroin in a matter of weeks. She thought we were stupid, but we weren't blind to what was going on. We knew our mom had issues, but we still loved her despite those flaws. I mean, wasn't a parent and child supposed to have unconditional love for each other? We certainly did.

After what happened here tonight, I was ready to get the fuck out of here and go back to the life we had made for ourselves in Atlanta, Georgia! At twenty years old, I was starting my junior year at Clark Atlanta University! As I looked around the place I called home my entire life, all I could think about was getting back to my dorm room on campus.

Nobody in these projects expected me or my sisters to leave the state and go to college somewhere else. They just assumed we'd take after our mom and be this welfare, food stamp, Section

8 recipient forever. Not a chance! Not after the way we grew up!

Me and my sisters had the brains to get us out and we were determined to leave this dump. So, as smart as we were, we were putting it to use to help us get the hell out of the projects and never look back.

My hope was that when we were done with school and had good jobs, we could get our mom into a rehab facility, but after what happened here tonight, she needed to realize that now was the time and that it was in her best interest.

I had two sisters, both older than I was. Saderia was the oldest at twenty- three. She had just graduated from Clark Atlanta last year with a degree in engineering. My sister Zaria was the middle child, and she had just turned twenty- one. She was in her first semester of her senior year with a major in criminology.

I thanked God every day for my sisters because I didn't know what I'd do without them. We were thicker than thieves at Walmart and tighter than a fat lady's pumps that were two sizes too small. Those two were my everything.

Our mom had a bad drug problem ever since I could remember, so me and my sisters had learned to depend on each other for everything. Saderia used to comb me and Zaria's hair for us to go to school. Most of the times we went to school hungry because mom would sell the food stamps for her drugs. So, usually by the middle of the month, we were out of food and had to wait for her stamps to come in the following month.

When Saderia was twelve, she started snatching little cakes and stuff from the corner store. By the way the old store owner would look at us, I had a feeling that he knew what she was doing. I think because of how we were dressed, he knew we were struggling, so he felt sorry for us. We were lucky that no one called CPS on my mom, but sometimes I wished someone had cared enough to report her. We deserved better than the crap we got from our mom, but one thing we didn't lack at home was love.

The struggle was real back then, and that was why me and my sisters worked hard to get scholarships to continue our education outside of Texas.

We loved our mom, and we never doubted that she loved us. Even though she did some unspeakable things to get money to support her habit, we knew that she was sick and couldn't help the shit she did. When my two older sisters tried to talk to her about it, she waved them off like they were wrong or something. Had she seen things from our eyes, she would have known that we were scared and felt like we were in danger. I mean, what kid wanted strange men coming into their home all hours of the night?

I knew we didn't like that shit, but since she was the parent and we were the kids, she basically told us if we didn't like what she did we could move out. How the hell did she expect us to move out when we were kids?

Me and my sisters were some bad ass chicks and everybody in the neighborhood knew it! We all had the same texture of hair, the same skin complexions and the same sparkling gray eyes. Me and my sister Zaria were the same height, but Saderia was a couple of inches taller than us. Zaria and I were only 5'6 but Saderia had long legs like a gazelle, so she stood at 5'8. Our skin was clear of any blemishes and acne.

I had a small beauty mark over the top corner of my upper lip on the right side, which at one time, I thought was a hideous blemish. It took me a while to grow into it, but I like it now. Zaria had a small space between her two front teeth, but it wasn't big enough to call it a gap. Saderia's skin and teeth were perfect and flawless.

I had been braiding hair since I was eight years old and now that I was older, I slayed! What I wanted to do one day was purchase my own hair salon and become a celebrity stylist. That was why I majored in business while continuing to do hair on the side.

I wanted to make sure that once I graduated, I would know how to handle and run my own shop. I used to have a work/ study job on campus, but then I discovered that I could make more money doing the other students' hair. Depending on what they wanted done to their hair, I could make as much as five hundred bucks a head. Most of those girls' money was coming in from their parents or boyfriends.

I didn't care where they got it from. As long as they could afford to pay for the service. Saderia's boyfriend, Alonzo told us that when we got back to Atlanta, he would have an apartment waiting for us. I was excited about that. Not because I didn't like living in the dormitory, but just because I would rather me and my sisters be back together again.

Alonzo was a street dude, who definitely handled business where my sister was concerned. He gave her money, bought her gifts and expensive handbags and he recently gave her a car when she graduated, an all- black Toyota Camry with tinted windows and a sunroof. Even the rims were black and what set her vehicle apart from the other ones like that was her seats. Alonzo had customized them in her favorite color, baby blue, and her initials were engraved in the driver's seat.

Alonzo was a few years older than Saderia at twenty- eight, if I wasn't mistaken about that. They were the perfect power couple and I hoped when I became involved with someone, he would take care of me the way Alonzo was taking care of my sister. Ever since my sister started dating him, we had been living a totally different lifestyle than the one we grew up in.

He took us to fancy restaurants, bought my sister designer clothes and expensive handbags. I had yet to meet the man of my dreams. At twenty years old, I wasn't ashamed to say that I was still a virgin because I was proud that I wasn't one of those girls who went around giving her goodies to anyone who said they loved me.

As we rushed over to the hospital to make sure our mom was okay, I said a prayer that she was. She was so damn weak when they wheeled her out of the bedroom. That man had given her a serious beat down.

Her face looked like cooked spinach. I almost felt sorry for her, but she knew better. We been telling her that inviting strangers here wasn't good for her. As I sat in the back seat of Saderia's rental car, I checked the time on my phone.

"Now you know this don't make no sense," I huffed. "It's almost one o'clock in the damn morning and we headed to the hospital cuz our mom got beat up by some fat john!"

"Right! But you got him good with that taser though sis," Zaria said as she cracked up.

"Fa real! Had it been me, I would've zapped his lil ding dong!" Saderia clowned. "That fuckin' bitch!"

"Ugh! Hell naw! I didn't want that nastiness on my taser! I'd never be able to use it the same way again," I retorted as I laughed.

"Y'all what is wrong with mom, bruh?!" Zaria questioned. "Her behavior is getting more and more erratic and dangerous!"

"I know," Saderia agreed with a sad expression.

"And the crazy thing about it is that we're not even in this damn state to keep an eye on her!" Zaria continued. "I don't know about y'all, but I'm tired of this shit and something has got to change!"

She was right. But no matter how we felt or where we were, mom had made it very clear that she did not intend to change in any way.

Chapter two

Saderia Bacardi

That was some crazy ass shit. I had just gotten out of the shower when I heard all the chaos going on in my mom's bedroom. I rushed in to see what was going on and found a naked man on the floor jumping around like a fish out of water. The taser that sat on the nightstand let me know that my sister had zapped his ass. Good for her!

Zaria rushed in and Jerrika hollered for us to call for help I left that up to Zaria as I rushed over to where my sister and mom were to check on them.

"What the hell happened?" I asked.

"This bozo..." Jerrika spewed angrily as she grabbed her taser and zapped his ass again. He moaned and winced as his body shook furiously.

"Stop girl! You gon kill him!" I yelled as I pushed her hand away from the man.

"Good! Do you see what he did to mom?" she cried as she jumped up and left the room.

"What the fuck happened ma?" I asked.

She mumbled something that I couldn't understand as Jerrika reentered the room with a bucket and towel.

"That nigga was pounding her face in when I walked in!" Jerrika explained.

"Oh, hell naw!" I spoke as my anger rose.

"Hell yes!" Jerrika confirmed.

Our mom was so badly beaten that the paramedics had to leave with her. I couldn't believe this shit but didn't really know why I was shocked. This was the type of shit mom had been getting into the whole time we had been here. This past week had been a week of nothing but men coming in and out of the tiny apartment.

I, myself, had caught her with at least three different men. The one on the floor was a whole new one. I knew my mom had a drug problem because she always had one, but this right here was something totally different. She had never brought men home with her like this before... or maybe she had and we just didn't know about it.

My mom's relationship with drugs was why when I first met Alonzo and found out what he did for a living, I wanted nothing to do with him. Even though he hadn't personally sold any drugs to my mom, someone just like him did. For that reason, I couldn't be with him.

However, he pursued and wooed me and wore me down with all his attention and expensive gifts. Over the past year, Alonzo had shown me the lifestyle that I had been dreaming about. The lifestyle I left home to find. Last week, Alonzo asked me to move in with him. As tempting as that was, I didn't think I should leave my sisters to fend for themselves just yet. I had graduated from college, but between the two of them, they still had a few years to go.

As I pulled into the parking lot of the hospital behind the ambulance, I quickly found a spot to park the car. Then we rushed into the emergency room to find out what the extent of our mom's injuries were. I wished we could sign her ass up for rehab because I knew as long as she had access to drugs, she was never going to change her ways.

"My name is Saderia Bacardi and we're here for our mom, Marie Bacardi. She was just brought in by ambulance as the victim of an assault," I explained to the female at the desk.

"Well, if she was just brought in, you'll need to give the doctors a chance to do an assessment of the patient. Just have a seat in the waiting room and someone should be out to see for y'all in a few minutes," she said.

"Okay. A few minutes," I stated sternly.

"Yes ma'am," she said with a tight smile.

As hard as that was for me and my sisters to walk away from the desk, we did and went to sit down in the waiting room. About fifteen minutes later, a nurse walked in looking for the family of Marie Bacardi. Me and my sisters rushed over to her.

"How's our mom?" I asked.

"I can take you to her. The doctor is waiting to speak with you," she said.

She turned and we followed her to the emergency area where the patients were being kept. She pushed open ER room thirteen and mom was hooked up to oxygen, monitors and IV. She looked even worse than when we saw her at home. Her face was extremely swollen to the point that she was almost unrecognizable.

If I didn't know that was my mom lying in that bed, I would have thought it was someone else.

"Hello ladies, I'm Dr. Randall. I am the ER physician on duty," the doctor said as he introduced himself to us.

"Nice to meet you, Dr. Randall. What's going on with our mom?" I asked, wanting him to get straight to the point.

"Well, as I told her, she has multiple contusions to her face and the blood vessel in her right eye was ruptured. I need to send her for a CT scan to see what we're dealing with as far as any head injuries. Once we get the results of the scan back, I will know how to proceed with treatment. I've also ordered blood work and an EKG to make sure she doesn't have any other issues going on. I will say this though, regardless of what the CT shows, your mother will need to be admitted to the hospital for at least three days because of the seriousness of the injuries to her face," Dr. Randall explained.

"Uhm uhm!" mom mumbled in an effort to decline.

I knew she was only thinking about her drugs and what would happen to her if she had to be admitted for that long, but that wasn't my concern. The doctors needed to do whatever was necessary to make her feel better, and if that meant she was going to come down off that high, so be it.

"Dr. Randall, please don't pay her any attention. She doesn't want to be admitted because our mom is a heroin addict. I'm sure she only wants to leave so she can go back to doing what she always does," I explained.

"Well, it'll be at least a couple of days before she's released. Thank you for letting me know about her problem with heroin. We don't want to prescribe her anything that will make her condition worse."

"I can't," mom weakly responded.

"Ms. Bacardi, you don't have a choice ma'am. There is no way I can discharge you until I can give you a clean bill of health, and I can't do that right now," Dr. Randall said.

"Can't stay," she responded weakly.

"You don't have a choice mom!" I stated as I shook my head from side to side. "You have to stay if you wanna feel better."

"Yea, mom! You have to stay!" Zaria cosigned.

"Well, someone should be coming in to get her for the CT scan. I also ordered lab work, so a nurse should be coming to draw her blood as well," Dr. Randall said.

"Thank you, Dr. Randall."

"No problem. I'll be back to check on your mom once the tests results come in," he said.

"I can't stay," mom mumbled.

"Why you always gotta make shit so hard?!" Zaria asked with an attitude. I could tell that she was pissed off... more than me and Jerrika were.

"You can and you will stay!" I spoke firmly. "That man whooped yo ass mama! You need to stay and let these people help you get right, and I'm not just talking about with your face and head either!"

"Yea mama," Jerrika said. She pulled out her phone and snapped a picture before turning it to our mom for her to see. "They say a picture is worth a thousand words."

As soon as she saw her face, she started to cry. I knew the salt from her tears were burning her open wounds, so I grabbed a tissue and wiped her eyes. Someone walked in with a wheelchair to take her for the CT scan. After helping her into the chair, he pushed her out the door.

"I need to call Alonzo," I said.

"It's 1:30 in the morning!" Zaria shrieked.

"And! I need to let him know what's going on because we may not be back in Atlanta until the weekend."

"Yea, I don't think we will be back until the weekend. As long as we're back before school starts Monday," Zaria said.

"Right," Jerrika said.

"Let me call Alonzo. He'll know what to do," I said as I stepped out of the room.

"Hello," he answered sounding like he was asleep.

"Babe, wake up!" I cried.

"I'm up! I'm up!" he stated. "What's going on? Are you alright?"

"No!" I whined.

"What happened?"

"My mom is in the hospital," I cried.

"What?! What the hell happened?"

"Some nigga she brought over to the crib whooped her ass! BAD!!"

"Aw shit! You know who he is?" he asked.

"I don't know him, but the police hauled him off to jail. Jerrika zapped him a couple of times with her taser!" I explained.

"Alright Jerrika!" he cheered.

"Yea, I'm glad she thought to grab it before she went to check on mom," I said.

"So, how bad is your mom's injuries?"

"Really bad! Her face is fucked up beyond recognition! She doesn't even look like our mom at all!"

"Aw man! Sorry to hear that babe. What you need me to do?"

"I need you to help me figure shit out! I can't possibly leave my mom while she's in the hospital!"

"Well, your sisters don't start class 'til next week right?"

"Yea."

"So, are all of y'all gonna stay out there with your mom?" Alonzo asked.

"Well yea! I am gonna try to convince her to check herself in rehab. At least if she does that, we won't have to worry about her for a while. But she's refusing!" I explained.

"Damn!" Alonzo expressed.

"I know right! She's being so fucking difficult, and Zaria is ready to just leave her here!"

"Well, I'm sure she's as frustrated as you are, babe."

"I am frustrated, but she's our mom! She's the only one we have," I said.

"Yea, I get that. Sounds like you need some more support," he said.

"I need you," I whined.

He chuckled a bit then said, "How about this? How about I come up there with a couple of my guys tomorrow? We can hop on a plane and be there by noon."

"Really?"

"Yea. We can come up there and rent a couple of suites at the Four Seasons so y'all can have a place to relax when y'all ain't at the hospital," he suggested.

"We need to go by my mom's place to get our things," I said.

"I'll get a rental car from the airport," he said.

"I already got one," I said.

"Babe, we can't all use the same vehicle."

"True. Sorry."

"No worries."

"I guess that sounds like a plan. What time are y'all gonna leave?" I asked.

"I gotta hit up my guys to make sure they can roll with me. Once I find that out, I can book the flights. Gimme a few minutes to pull this shit together, and I'ma hit you back."

"Okay. Thanks bae. I love you."

"I love you too."

We ended the call, and I went back to the room to tell my sisters about Alonzo's plan to come out here to meet us.

Chapter three

Alonzo 'Zo' Lopez

I did not expect my girl to hit me up this late, so for her to be calling me at 1:33 in the morning, I knew something was wrong. I picked up the phone and once I ended the call with 'I love you', I felt the pop upside my head. I immediately jumped out of bed and started putting my clothes on.

"What the fuck you hit me for?" I asked.

"Nigga you got nerve to ask me that after you just laid in my hotel bed and told that girl you love her!"

"Shit, I ain't lie!"

"Wooooow! You really gon do me like that!"

"What did I do though? I wasn't gon just let her say that she loved me and leave her hanging! All that was gon do was cause problems in our relationship!" I explained with a puzzled expression on my face. The nerve of her to think that shit!

"Wooooow! So, that's it? You running to go see about her ass!"

"Fuckin' right!" I responded.

"I did not fly out here so you can fly out there!" Sina argued.

"I didn't ask you to fly out here!"

"You didn't exactly tell me to go back home either!" she whined.

"Go back home!" I proclaimed.

"I wish you had told me that sooner," she said as she pouted. "Like before we had sex!"

"Aye, you called and told me you were here and asked me to come by to talk. As a courtesy cuz you flew all the way from NYC, that's what I did! I came by to talk, but you showed up at the door in your birthday suit, so I reacted."

"That's what this was? A fucking reaction!"

"Aye, I'm a man before anything else! So, yes, I reacted to your naked ass cuz you sexy as fuck!" I stated as I shrugged my shoulders.

"So, at 1:37 in the morning, you're just gonna leave me here by myself to go chase after that bitch!"

"Aye, watch yo fuckin' mouth when you talking about my girl nah! You knew what time it was when you brought yo ass down here! That's why you showed up at the door with yo ass and titties out! Don't get mad and disrespect my girl cuz shit ain't worked out the way you wanted them to! You threw the puddy at me, I took it, and now I'm out!" I stated as I chucked the deuces.

"Woooow! I wonder what "your girl" would say if she knew we just had sex," she threatened.

"Don't do that," I said as I sneered at her.

"Don't do what?"

"Write a check yo ass ain't prepared to cash."

"Says who?" she asked with a smirk as she reached for her phone that was on the nightstand.

"Look Sina, the bottom line is you shouldn't have flown out here! You knew I had a girl and we was in a relationship. Now you mad cuz I gotta go see for her. Mad for what though?"

"I thought we were working things out..." she whined as tears streamed from her eyes.

"Why though?"

"Cuz we just had sex MORON!!"

"I'm the moron, but you're the one crying cuz I don't wanna be with you. Yea, okay," I clowned as I stuck my feet in my Jordan's.

"This is funny to you!" she cried as she tossed the TV remote at me.

"It is actually," I said as I released another chuckle. "You mad cuz you played yo'self. That's the shit that's got me laughing."

"Well, you won't find it so funny when I call that bitch and tell her about our little romp in my hotel bed," she threatened.

"Aye, do what you wanna do. Telling her won't make you feel better cuz I still won't be with yo ass!" Her mouth dropped open, and she stared at me with a hurt expression. "What? Why you looking at me like that? You know for a fact that we weren't good together. We broke up for a reason, and I ain't looking to go backwards. I've moved on, so you should do the same Sina!" I begged. "I ain't gon even lie to you. Even if I was single, I wouldn't be with you cuz I don't love you no more."

"Wow! That wasn't what you said earlier!"

"Girl you crazy!" I laughed out loud. "I did not tell you that I loved you!"

"No, maybe not with your mouth but when you made love to me, you did," she said with a smile.

"Girl we didn't make love. We FUCKED! And the sex wasn't even all that either. I mean, nothing to go around bragging about to nobody! But do whatever you wanna do. I'ma never gonna be with you, especially after those threats you just made. Now, I'ma tell you this for the last time, so I hope you got your listening cap on. Don't fly out here no more to see me cuz I moved on! I got a girl that I really love and don't want you no more! Comprende!"

"Uh huh! I comprende alright," she stated in an arrogantly smug tone.

I wasn't worried about Sina telling Saderia anything about this little episode, and if she did, I knew how to clean that shit with my girl right up. I wasn't even worried about this bitch right here.

Without another fucking word, I walked out of the hotel room and hit up my boys, Rocky and Gotti. I explained the situation to them and of course, they were willing to roll out with me. Once I got that taken care of, I went online and booked the three of us first- class tickets to Houston so I could go see about my baby. I had decided to bring Gotti because he was my right- hand. I also knew that him and Zaria were sweet on each other and figured she would need him.

Rocky had been working for me about three years ago, and he was like a little brother to me. He and Gotti were definitely family as far as I was concerned. I would kill for these niggas. It took a lot for me to trust people and they both had earned it. Rocky was only twenty- three, but he had proven himself worthy a long time ago.

With his light skin and green eyes, no one expected him to be as cold- blooded as he was. That lil nigga even surprised me with that shit. Once I made it back to my crib, I jumped in the shower to wash off Sina's scent. I couldn't believe I had allowed her to set me back that way. I wasn't going to worry about her idle threats to tell Saderia about us because I knew she didn't have the balls she thought she did.

Sina wanted me, and she knew if she opened that can of worms and mentioned this little night to my girl, she would shut the door on that dream of her becoming Mrs. Alonzo Lopez for good. Shit, she could say goodbye to that shit anyway because I was focused on giving that title to Saderia. She was a real one and she deserved to be my wife.

Sina had betrayed me back when we were dating, and I swore that she would never get the chance to fuck over me again. I ended things with her five years ago, and she still hadn't given up on the two of us getting back together. No matter how many times I told her that it would never happen because I couldn't trust her, she refused to give up.

I should've never gone to that hotel, especially since she showed up unannounced and uninvited. After I got out of the shower, I packed a quick bag since our flight was scheduled to leave at 10:15 in the morning. Then I climbed in between these thousand- thread count Egyptian cotton sheets and fell right to sleep.

The next morning, I woke up and got dressed. I hit up my boys to let them know I was about to head their way. I grabbed my bag and made my way to the front door. After securing the alarm and locking the door, I got in the awaiting Chevy Suburban. After the guy put my bag in the back, he climbed in behind the wheel and went to scoop up Gotti.

After I swung by Gotti's crib, the driver headed to Rocky's condo. "Man, sorry to hear about the girls' mom," Gotti expressed sadly.

"Yea, that shit sucks! Saderia is all worried and shit. They'll probably be there with their mom until the weekend, so I hope you don't have anything planned," I explained.

"Nah, I'm good 'til next week. I tried calling Zaria, but she didn't answer."

"She was probably asleep or had her phone on DND," I surmised. "I mean, Saderia did say their mom was getting admitted to the hospital. I'm sure they all had a long night."

"Speaking of long night..."

"I don't even wanna talk about it!"

"Dude don't tell me you slept with Sina!"

"Man, I wasn't planning to, but she showed up at the door butt ass naked!" I said in an effort to try to defend my actions.

"I told you it was a trap, and you shouldn't go! I warned you that going over there was a mistake."

"Man, I wish I had listened!"

"Yea, now you wish you listened. Don't we always say that shit after we do the wrong damn thing?" Gotti questioned.

"Man, that shit wasn't my fault!"

The driver pulled up to Rocky's place and he hopped in. After greeting us with handshakes, he asked, "Why y'all look so sad? Don't tell me their mom passed!"

"Nah, at least not that we know of," I said.

"Good. I would hate to hear that shit. Chicks need their moms, ya know?"

"Yea, I know," I agreed as I nodded my head.

"Thanks for inviting me to tag along. I been wanting to get at yo sis in law for a minute now," Rocky admitted.

"Which sister?" Gotti asked with a raised brow and smirk.

"Not the one you with!" Rocky quipped. "I like the baby sister."

"Yea, you better be careful with the baby. You fuck around and hurt her feelings, dem other two gon fuck you up!" I stated with a laugh.

"Damn! It's like that!" Rocky asked.

"Nigga, they ride hard for one another. You fuck over one, you fuck over all of 'em!" I concluded.

The more I sat and thought about that shit, the more I realized that what I had done last night was just as bad or worse than anything Rocky could do. Me and my girl have been together for a while now. Rocky and Jerrika weren't even an item yet. If Saderia ever found out about what me and Sina did last night...

Twenty minutes later, the driver pulled up to Hartsfield Jackson Atlanta Airport. He put the truck in 'park' and opened the back doors to let us out. Then he made his way to the rear of the truck and began to pull out our bags. I handed him a fifty- dollar bill and thanked him for the ride. Once we had checked in, we waited about fifteen minutes for them to announce that our flight was boarding.

I hadn't been to Houston in a long time. I definitely wished it were under better circumstances, but maybe me and my girl would be able to sneak away for lunch and a little shopping at the Galleria Mall. I wasn't going to count on that too much though because I knew we were here to support them concerning their mom.

The way it was now almost felt like we were going to a funeral. I relaxed once the plane was in the air, but it didn't take long for us to descend and reach our destination.

Whatever Saderia needed, I was going to be there for her, her mom and sisters too.

Chapter four

Zaria Bacardi

Our mom had been moved to a private room around four o'clock this morning and since only two visitors were allowed to stay with her, that meant one of us had to go. Me and Jerrika let Saderia stay with mom while we spent the rest of the night in the waiting room. Around eight this morning, my older sister greeted me and Jerrika with coffee from the cafeteria. As she sat in the chair next to us, I wiped the sleep from my eyes.

"How's mom?" Jerrika asked.

"Okay for now. She had a restless night and wanted to leave, but I told her that we needed her to stay and get better."

"She must be itching for those drugs," I commented as I shook my head.

"Well, she's sick sis. Until she gets help for her addiction, she's always gonna be in the same damn condition," Saderia stated.

"Where is she now?"

"They took her to cardiology for some tests on her heart. They wanna make sure it's functioning properly considering the abuse she has been putting her body through," my sister explained. "She also had a slight irregularity with her heartbeat."

"So, now they think there's something wrong with her heart," I said.

"Maybe. They aren't saying much, but I'm sure her heart isn't functioning right considering..."

"Damn! I don't want anything bad to happen to mama!" Jerrika cried.

"Define bad, little sister cuz something bad has been happening to mama," I stated.

"Well, I don't want her to die!" Jerrika added.

"Unfortunately, it's not up to us," Saderia said in a low tone. "Mama has to want to do better and make certain life changes that she hasn't been able to agree to before. She's gonna have to kick the drug habit and enter a rehab program. That's the only way she'll be able to save herself."

"Damn! Then we might as well go shopping for our black dresses now!" I stated.

"Don't say that!" Jerrika cried.

"Jerrika, stop acting so naïve. You're not a child anymore! You know what mom is up against, so unless she gets her shit together, she is going to die!" I retorted angrily.

I wasn't angry with my sister. I was angry with our mom because how the hell could she allow shit to get this fucking bad with her health? Why didn't she care enough about us to do better? If she didn't want to live for herself, why not live for us? Me and my sisters had been doing everything we could to make her proud, and she had been doing everything she could to make us ashamed of her.

The universe worked in a crazy way, and I didn't like that shit at all.

"Have you heard from Alonzo? Is he still coming?" I asked in an effort to talk about something else.

"No, I haven't heard from him yet. I'm sure he'll text me before they get on the plane," Saderia said.

"Who is they? Who is he bringing down here with him?" I asked curiously with a raised eyebrow.

"I'm not sure. He didn't tell me. I'm sure Gotti is coming though, if that's what you wanna know," Saderia responded.

"Speaking of Gotti. He called me not too long ago, but I was knocked out in this uncomfortable ass chair!" I informed them.

"Well, you can call him back to see what he wanted," Jerrika suggested.

"Nope. If he's coming here, I'll just wait until he gets here to talk to him," I said.

I didn't chase men. Men chased me all day, every day. Although me and Gotti weren't a couple yet, we had gone out a few times. I enjoyed the time we spent together, but I got the feeling that he was a player, and I wasn't trying to be another notch on his damn belt.

"Well, y'all can come in mom's room if y'all want to," Saderia said.

"I thought only two visitors were allowed at a time," I said.

"Well, we're three sisters, so if they put one out, they'll have to throw us all out!" She smirked.

So, the three of us headed to the room. When we got there, our mom still hadn't come back yet. Ten minutes later, they wheeled her into the room. Damn! Her face looked worse than yesterday!

Her eyes were swollen shut. She had a deep cut on her forehead over her right eye which had been stitched. She had a cut on her left cheek that also had stitches. Both her lips were busted, and she was missing three teeth. She just looked really bad.

"Hey mom," I greeted as Jerrika waved. "How do you feel?"

"Like I've been run over by a dump truck!" she stated as she grimaced in pain.

If she only knew she looked exactly how she felt too!

Two hours after the test, the doctor walked in with a perplexed expression on his face. "I'm glad you all are here because I need to talk to you about the tests we performed on your mom."

"Is she okay?" Jerrika asked.

"Well, the reason she was sent to the cardiologist was because she had an abnormal rhythm. The cardiologist will be here in a minute to discuss his findings..."

The door opened soon after and another doctor walked in. "Hello, Dr. Walker. I was just letting the family know that you were on your way to discuss Ms. Bacardi's results," Dr. Grant explained.

"Is our mom gonna be okay?" I asked.

"Your mom has an irregular heart rhythm which concerned me and Dr. Grant. That was why I wanted to perform the test to find out how severe the issue is. Your mom has developed a condition called endocarditis, which can be very serious if you continue down the path you are going with the drug use, Ms. Bacardi," Dr. Walker explained.

"So, if she stops using today, will her heart be okay?" I asked.

"With the proper antibiotics, the infection can be cleared up in a few days, so we'll start her on it, ASAP. Should she continue the path she's already on, it could lead to a heart attack, stroke, or worse, complete heart failure. Now, we have a rehab facility in this hospital, and once I clear up the infection, I can transfer her up to the eighth floor. She would have to sign off to receive the treatment though," he explained.

"Uhm uhm," mom mumbled as she shook her head from side to side.

"Mom, you have to stay! Did you hear what the doctor said?" Saderia asked.

"Do you wanna die mom?" Jerrika asked with tears in her eyes.

"I can't," mom said.

"Well, I'm gonna leave the four of you to discuss your options. Just know that if your mom doesn't get help soon, her condition will eventually worsen," Dr. Grant said.

"I thought you said you would give her the antibiotics," Jerrika said with a worried tone.

"The infection will heal, but if she continues to use drugs, it will return and the next time... well, I won't speak negatively. I just hope you make the right choice Ms. Bacardi," Dr. Grant said as he and Dr. Walker turned and left the room.

"Mom, I know you don't want to stay in the hospital, but you have an infection that requires antibiotics to help you recover. Once you're done with that, you need to check into the rehab..."

"NO!" She was pretty adamant that she didn't want to go to rehab, which pissed me off.

She seemed to be only concerned with herself. I thought when people became parents, they were supposed to put their kids first. She never did that! She always put herself before me and my sisters and I was sick of it!

"I can't do this shit!" I fumed. "If she wants to kill herself, let her! But I won't be around to watch this shit! You hear that mom?! If you don't go to rehab, I'm gonna go back to Atlanta and not come back to visit again!"

She laid in bed and shrugged her shoulders like she didn't care. "See! She doesn't give a fuck how we feel! All she cares about is getting high and floating on a fucking cloud!" By this time, I was livid.

"ZARIA!! You aren't helping!" Saderia fussed with an attitude.

"Whatever! I cannot with her!" I stated and stormed out of the room.

I headed to the waiting room to wait for my sisters to eventually join me. I loved my mom, but she was pissing me off with her attitude! I wanted to live, so if the doctors came at me with a choice to live or die, I would make the choice that would give me the longest life and more time with my family. Not our mom!

She was only interesting in making the choice that was best for her and what she wanted. I paced the floor of the waiting room for about ten minutes when the door opened and Alonzo, Gotti and Rocky walked in.

"Hey," Alonzo greeted me with a warm hug. "How's your mom?"

"Being stubborn as fuck as always! Hey y'all," I greeted Gotti and Rocky.

"C'mon now. I know you can do better than that and it looks like you could use one of these," Gotti said as he pulled me into his strong arms for a bear hug.

I had to admit that after everything I had been going through over the past few hours, it felt good to be held by him. Gotti was tall, about 6'1, had pretty brown eyes, nice thick lips, a smooth caramel skin tone and he smelled refreshing and edible... or maybe I was just hungry since I hadn't eaten all day.

"Okay, that's enough," I said as I pushed myself out of his arms.

"Where's your sister?" Alonzo asked.

"In the room trying to convince my mom to let these doctors admit her into rehab," I explained.

"Can you go let her know that I'm here please?" he asked.

"Yea."

I pulled myself away from Gotti who had his arm draped across my shoulders. I walked away making sure to twitch my hips just a little harder because I knew Gotti was watching me. I went to the room and pushed the door open.

"Alonzo here," I announced.

I could see the stress immediately leave Saderia's face as she smiled and jumped up. "I'll be back mom!" she said as she headed towards the door. The two of us walked out, leaving Jerrika to deal with mom on her own.

"You do know as long as you and Jerrika baby mom, she's never gonna do what she needs to do to get better," I said as I side eyed my older sister.

"So, what do you want me to do Zaria?" she asked. "You want me to do what you did and turn my back on her?"

"I ain't saying all that but y'all definitely need to put y'all feet down!"

"So, you were serious when you said you wouldn't visit her if she doesn't go to rehab?" Saderia asked.

"Dead ass! Play with her if you want to, but I ain't!" I replied angrily as I rolled my eyes.

We walked into the waiting room, and she flew into Alonzo's arms. While they talked and Alonzo comforted her, Gotti walked over to me to check on me.

"Yo, you good?"

"No, but thanks for asking."

"You wanna talk about it?" he asked with concern on his face.

"Not right now, thank you."

"No problem. Just know I'm here if you need anything," he said.

"Shit, I'm hungry," I admitted with a smirk.

"Say less! You wanna go down to the cafeteria or you wanna go eat somewhere?"

"I don't want any hospital food."

"Okay, cool. Lemme get the keys for the rental from Alonzo, and we can dip," he said.

"Cool."

To be honest, I just wanted to get out of this damn hospital. My mom wasn't thinking straight and this whole situation was stressful as fuck. Gotti was smelling all good and shit, so I wasn't sure if being alone with him was a good idea, but I didn't care. I just needed some time away from here.

I watched as Alonzo handed him the keys and he turned towards me and stretched out his hand. I walked over and slipped my hand in his and we headed to the elevators. We were quiet on the ride down, mostly because I didn't trust myself to speak. Once we made it to the first floor, he held my hand to the parking lot.

He unlocked the SUV and opened the door for me to hop into the passenger's seat. He climbed into the driver's seat and turned to look at me.

"Where to?"

"I don't know. Somewhere quiet," I said.

"Sssshhhiiid! Say less," he said.

He started the truck and merged onto the highway. As I relaxed in the comfortable leather seat, I closed my eyes and listened to the smooth sounds of Ciara flowing through the speakers. I didn't even know I had fallen asleep until Gotti nudged me.

"What? Where are we?" I asked as we sat outside what looked like a hotel parking lot.

"The Four Seasons," he said.

"Oh, uh uh!" I looked at him sideways.

"Hear me out. You said you wanted to go somewhere quiet, so I brought you here because we have rooms here. I figured we could chill out and order room service. I know you're probably thinking I brought you here to have sex, but that's not what's on my mind right now. Honestly," he said.

Shit, it might not have been on his mind but it was definitely on mine. I didn't trust myself being alone with Gotti, but he had brought me here because I wanted peace and quiet.

"If you don't wanna stay, I'll gladly take you to some fast- food joint or a crowded restaurant."

"No, I for sure don't want that! We can go in but if you try anything..."

"I won't," he promised.

"Fine," I said.

He turned the truck off and walked around to open the door. He held his hand out to help me out of the truck and together we walked inside the hotel. I had never been to The Four Seasons before, so I was instantly wowed. The high ceilings and gorgeous chandeliers caused my mouth to drop.

As I looked around the gorgeous and expensive hotel, Gotti took my hand and led me towards the elevator. He pressed the button for the sixth floor and stood behind me with his arms draped across me. It looked like we were a couple even though we weren't.

The elevator dinged and we stepped off. He held my hand and led me to his room. He put the key in the lock and when the light turned green, he pushed the door open.

I walked in and once again, my mouth hit the floor. This was no ordinary room. It had a living room, a kitchenette, a sitting area by the balcony, a huge bathroom, and an actual bedroom.

"Oh my God!" I gawked.

"You like the suite?" he asked.

"Of course, I like the suite! What's not to like?" I questioned. "I ain't never been in no hotel as nice as this before!"

"Never?" Gotti inquired with a raised eyebrow.

"NEVER!" I confirmed.

"Whenever we go out of town, we stay in hotels like this all the time," he stated with a smile. He grabbed the menu off the dresser and handed it to me. "Check to see what you would like to order."

I stared at the menu and decided on a bacon cheeseburger with fries. "Out of everything on that menu, you want a hamburger!"

"Not just any hamburger... a bacon cheeseburger. There's a difference," I replied with a smile.

"Okay. I'll put the order in."

"I wish I could take a shower," I said as I rolled my neck while trying to get the kinks out from last night's bad sleeping arrangement.

"Why can't you?" Gotti asked.

"I don't have any clothes here!"

"So!" He shrugged. "There's an extra robe in the bathroom that you..."

"Uh uh! No sir!" I interjected as I wagged my finger.

"What?!" he asked with a sheepish grin.

"You are not about to get me naked in this room!"

"What? You don't think I can control myself if you're naked?" he inquired.

"I don't think any man can control themselves if I get naked," I flirted.

"Ohhhhhh, okay! Well, I would be the first to prove you wrong," he stated.

"There's a nice garden tub in there that I'd like to soak in," I admitted.

"Help yourself, baby girl."

I liked when he called me that. It made me feel giddy inside because Gotti was seven years older than me. I didn't mind that though because my grandmother used to always say that a man older than you would take care of you. So, if I ever got involved with a man on a serious relationship tip, it would be with someone older who had money and could not only take care of me but spoil the hell out of me since I missed that growing up.

I wanted to pass on the bath, but that tub was calling my name, so I went for it. "I won't be long," I promised.

"Take your time. There's some vanilla bubble bath in the bathroom on the counter," he said.

"You had a bitch in here already!" I frowned.

"No! I bought that shit for me!"

"You like taking bubble baths!"

"Why you think my skin feels like a baby's ass?" he teased with a wink.

"I am not about to play with you!" I laughed out loud as I walked towards the bathroom.

While I was in the bathroom running the water, I heard him on the phone with room service. I grabbed the bottle of bubble bath off the counter and poured some under the open faucet. As the bubbles filled the tub, the room filled with the aromatic fragrance of vanilla. I removed my clothes and stepped into the tub.

As I submerged my body in the bubbles, I turned the faucet off. As I thought about Gotti in the other room, I shook my head. I should not be in here, and I definitely shouldn't be naked. But this water felt so good that I couldn't help but relax.

Chapter five

Gage 'Gotti' Morrison

Of course, I came to Houston to check on Zaria. Even though we weren't an official couple, the two of us had been kicking it for a few months. For whatever reason, she had been holding out on having sex with me. It was cool because I always prided myself on how patient I was with women.

While Zaria took a bubble bath, I ordered food from room service. Once I finished with that, I hit up Alonzo to let him know that I wouldn't be returning right away.

Me: Hey bro, I'ma be a while. I'm at the hotel so if you need the truck lemme know and I'll bring it to you

A couple of minutes later, he hit me back.

Zo: Nah, we straight. Me and Rocky gon stick around for a couple of hours and then we gon use Saderia's rental to get us back to the hotel

Me: Oh, aight... cool. Lemme know if you change your mind and want the truck though.

Zo: I told you I'm straight bro. Handle ya business!

I chuckled a little before I responded.

Me: It ain't what you think bro... LOL!

Zo: Aye, that ain't my business! I'ma holla at you when I get back to the room!

Me: Cool

KNOCK! KNOCK! KNOCK!

I went to the door to answer it because I knew it was room service with our food. I opened the door, and the guy wheeled the cart into the room. I handed him a twenty- dollar tip and he headed back out the door. I waited for Zaria to come out of the bathroom before I ate because I wanted us to eat together. Five minutes after the waiter left, she walked into the living room area.

"Sorry I took so long. That bath was everything!" she expressed with a smile.

"No problem. I'm glad you enjoyed it," I said returning the smile. You smell good as fuck baby girl!"

"Just remember what you said," she warned.

"I know how to control myself." I chuckled as I patted the seat next to me on the sofa. "Come sit down."

As she took a seat, we lifted the domes off our food plates. "That's a good- looking burger!" Zaria said as she rubbed her hands together. "I'm about to tear that shit up!"

"Shoot! I know that's right."

"I almost feel guilty about eating cuz I know my sisters must be starving."

"Don't sweat it. I heard from Alonzo, and he said that they would be headed here in a couple of hours," I informed her.

"Oh, okay. I'ma have to text them to ask about mama," she said with a saddened expression on her beautiful face.

"Your mom doing that bad huh?"

"Man, I don't even wanna talk about her..."

"Okay. Just know I'm here if you do," I offered.

"I'm good. I came here to eat and get away from my worries. Not to continue stressing about it, so if it's all the same to you, I'd rather talk about something else. Like what made you come out here. I know you had something better to do than babysit me," Zaria surmised.

"You think I'm babysitting you? That ain't why I'm here," I said.

"Why are you here?"

"When I heard about your mom, and Zo asked me to roll with him, I didn't hesitate cuz I was worried about you."

"You could've called," she said.

"I did. You didn't answer," I reminded her.

"I was probably sleeping in that uncomfortable ass chair!"

"Well, you don't have to sleep in those chairs if you don't want to tonight," I offered. "And to answer your question, I'm here because I was concerned about you. I wanted to make sure that you were good... in person."

"Well, thank you," she said as she shoulder bumped me with a smile.

The more time I spent with Zaria, the more I liked her and wanted to be with her. I thought the two of us could be good in a relationship together, but that wasn't something she was interested in. I didn't want to force myself on her, so I'd just have to wait until she decided this was what she wanted.

After we were done eating, I covered the plates back and put them on the rolling cart. I wheeled them to the door and left it sitting outside the room. We sat on the sofa and chatted for about twenty minutes when I leaned over and kissed Zaria. I just knew she was about to push me away and slap me because she had warned me already, but she didn't stop me. I closed the gap between us and continued to kiss her as my hands roamed her body.

When I untied her bathrobe and opened it up, I was sure she was about to slap the shit out of me. When she didn't, I trailed my kisses from her lips to her neck. She moaned softly as I squeezed the tips of her nipples with my fingertips.

"Ooouuu!" she moaned.

I brought my mouth on her right boob and sucked it while my teeth gently grazed her nipple. I had no problem dropping to my knees and sucking on her sweetness. I had been wanting to do that shit for a while now. I dropped to my knees and spread her legs apart.

I stared up at her as she bit down on her bottom lip. I wanted her to watch me eat her pussy. I parted her lips and began to lick on her kitty. She dropped her head on the back of the sofa and closed her eyes as she moaned.

"Uh uh," I said. "I want you to watch me!"

She locked eyes with mine and I drove my tongue inside her. Her mouth opened a little as a moan escaped her pretty lips. I sucked her like I needed that honey for survival.

"Sssssss!" she hissed like a sexy snake. "Oh my God!"

When I felt her cream leaking on my tongue, I sucked her dry. I quickly removed my shirt and dropped my sweats as I climbed between her legs. I pulled her butt to the edge of the sofa and pushed my dick inside her.

She moaned and hissed as her pussy tried to accommodate the girth of my dick. It took several seconds to get the entire length of my dick inside her. She held on to my face as I buried my tongue in her mouth. After a couple of deep tongue thrusts, she broke the kiss and moaned louder. I braced myself and stood up with her sexy ass in my hand.

I pummeled deep inside her, over and over again. She held on to me until her body shivered and she started shaking. My guess was that she had another orgasm. I sat on the sofa with her in my lap.

She gyrated and rotated her hips against me like a professional belly dancer. I pulled her close to me for a kiss while I continued to plow my dick inside her moistened pussy like a jack hammer. I felt her body tense up again before she started to shiver. I removed my mouth from her sweet, soft lips and licked her vanilla scented neck. As she moaned deeply, my kisses moved to her perfectly plump D cup breasts.

My tongue ran circles around her areola as I wrapped my entire mouth around her breasts, one at a time. I sucked on those knockers like I was a titty milk sucking newborn. I felt her body tensing up again for another orgasm. That made number four or five to my none. It wasn't that I didn't want to cum, but her pussy felt so good, I wanted to give her more of this dick before I erupted.

By the time I was done with her, I wanted her to miss the hell out of me when we weren't together. That way, she would know that I was the nigga for her. After her body calmed down, I had her get on her hands and knees on the plush carpeted floor. I got behind her and pushed her back down a little to deepen the arch. With her butt in the air, I positioned myself behind her and slammed deep inside her soaking, wet kitty.

She moaned loudly as I pumped into her like a jackhammer. I wanted her to feel that dick in her chest. She began to scream with pleasure.

"Fuck me!" she yelled as I plunged deeper into that coochie. "Harder!"

Damn! She must not have had no dick in a long time, and since I aimed to please, I drove my dick so far inside her, she was trying to push me out. She had me fucked up and should have been careful what she asked for. I gripped her hips to keep her in place.

"Uh uh!" I said. "Move your hand!"

She kept her left hand on my thigh, so I removed it myself. Then I started going in that pussy harder, which was what she begged for. I was trying to drown in that coochie. By the time I was done with her, all she could do was collapse on the floor. She was breathing and panting really hard as I laid on the carpet next to her.

I rubbed her back while taking deep breaths in and exhaling. "You good?" I asked.

"Whew!" she expressed.

"Not hard enough?" I asked. She gave me a funny expression but didn't say anything. "Next time I'll go harder."

"Real funny," she expressed.

"Ha! HA!" I quipped.

"Who even said there was gonna be a next time?" she asked.

"Sssshhhiiid! The way that pussy was clapping for this dick! I have no doubt there will be a next time!"

"Uh huh," Zaria mumbled as she closed her eyes.

I wasn't crazy. She could say what she wanted to right now, but we both knew that we would be having sex again. She looked tired, so I stood up and reached for her hand.

"C'mon," I said. "Let's get off this floor and go in the bedroom."

"I need to go see about my mom."

"You need to rest. I can see how tired you are. Hit your sisters up and find out how your mom is doing and come like in this big ass bed and get you some rest..."

"I appreciate you Gotti, but..."

"No buts, Zaria. What good are you to anybody if you're sleeping on your feet?"

She remained quiet for a minute, then took my hand. I helped her off the floor and led her to the bedroom of the suite. I pulled the covers back and motioned for her to climb in. She did as she was told and slipped between the cool sheets. I covered her and within minutes, she was asleep.

I grabbed my phone and dialed up Zo. He answered on the second ring.

"Whaddup?"

"Aye, I was hitting you up to find out how Zaria's mom is doing," I inquired.

"She's good. I believe Saderia said they giving her some antibiotics for an infection she got..."

"Who is that?" Saderia asked.

"Gotti."

"Oh," she mumbled. "Ask him where is my sister."

"Tell her that her sister is fine. She's exhausted so I made her take a nap," I explained.

"Yea, I bet she is," Zo said with a chuckle.

"Nah bro, fa real! She said her and little sister slept in those hospital chairs in the waiting room all night..."

"Oh word!"

"Yea. I just wanted to make sure she was good, and since she wanted to go somewhere quiet, we came here. She ate and now she's sleeping," I explained, purposely leaving out the part about us having sex.

I wasn't sure how much Zaria wanted anybody to know about us, so until she decided she wanted to make our shit public, it would stay between us.

"Well, we all headed over to their mom's place to pick up their bags. Since their mom gon be in the hospital for a while, they gon just stay with us at the hotel," Zo explained.

"Oh, aight. That's cool. So, their mom is good then?"

"She's stable and on medication that keeps her drowsy. She took a pretty bad beating, so they trying to keep her sedated until the swelling goes down cuz she keeps talking about leaving," Zo went on to explain.

"Damn! I'm not surprised though considering she's addicted to drugs. That's how they are. Nothing and no one else matters but that fix."

"Yea, but look, we just got to their crib, so I'ma holla at you when we get back to the hotel."

"Y'all gon grab Zaria's shit too, right?"

"Well yea, dawg! She got clothes over there now?" Zo asked.

"Nah."

"Well, alright then! See you when we get back."

"Yea, aight."

We ended the call and I listened as smiled as Zaria snored softly. She was so fucking beautiful right now. To be honest, she looked just like an angel. I put my phone on the nightstand and was about to climb in the bed when I heard her phone ringing. I went to get it even though I probably shouldn't have.

I followed the ringing to the bathroom where she had left it on the counter. I picked it up and saw that it was some nigga named Dominic.

"Who the fuck is Dominic?" I inquired out loud to no one in particular.

The phone stopped ringing, then started again before I could put it back down on the counter. It was the same nigga! Everything in me was saying don't answer, but curiosity got the best of me.

"Whaddup?" I answered.

"Oh snap! I must have dialed the wrong number," he said.

"I don't think so since this yo second or third time calling," I remarked.

He was quiet for a couple of seconds before he responded. "You right. I just checked my phone and this is the right number, but who the hell are you?"

Aw shit! I just knew this nigga wasn't getting slick at the mouth with me. "Aye ma nigga, don't be asking me no shit about who I am. Worry 'bout who the fuck you are!"

"Where Zaria at?"

"She sleep."

"Oh, she sleep, huh? So, why the fuck you playin' on her damn phone?" he asked.

"Nigga, do I sound like a muthafuckin' child to you to be playin' on somebody phone?" I asked angrily. "You the one playin' on this damn line! Now, like I told you, Zaria sleeping, but when she wakes up I'ma let her know that you hit her up!"

"Nigga you ain't gotta let her know shit about me, you dig! You don't fuckin' know me!"

"Nigga fuck you! I ain't trying to get to know yo bitch ass!" I barked. "Matter fact, you ain't even gotta worry 'bout me telling her shit! And don't bother calling this phone no more cuz she ain't yo concern!"

"Nigga what?! You got me fucked up!"

"Nah homie! You got me fucked up, but aye, don't call this phone no more bitch!"

With that being said, I hung the phone up in his face. I didn't know her password to unlock the phone and block that nigga, so I turned her ringer off. Soon as I did that, his name popped up on the screen, so I swiped to ignore his call. I was heated now.

Who the fuck was that nigga? Was he some random ass nigga that Zaria was fucking while she had been down here in Houston. Was he the reason that she wasn't trying to get involved with me? Shit, whatever their relationship was before we had sex was definitely going to be over now.

I wasn't even going to worry about that nigga because he was no competition for me, no matter who he was. I put him out of my mind and climbed in bed next to Zaria. I pulled her close to me and snuggled up with her. This was the most intimate that she and I had ever gotten.

Whatever was holding her back before, I was glad she had let her guard down earlier. I kissed her forehead before I closed my eyes and soon fell asleep.

BANG! BANG! BANG!

"Who in the world..." I mumbled as I tried to figure out what the hell was going on.

BANG! BANG! BANG!

"What's going on?" Zaria asked in a groggy tone.

"I'on know. Somebody banging on my fucking door like the police!" I slipped my boxers and pants on and headed for the door. "Stay there!"

"ZARIA!!" I heard a nigga's voice on the other side of the door. It sounded like the same fool I was arguing with on the phone.

BANG! BANG! BANG!

"Oh my God! What the hell?!" she questioned.

"Yea, what the hell!" I repeated as I went to the door. I peeked through the peephole and saw an angry nigga on the other side.

"Don't open it!" Zaria shrieked.

"Bullshit! Some nigga comes banging on my fucking door, you best believe I'ma open it!"

"How did he know that I was here?"

"You tell me!" I expressed as I pulled the door back. The nigga looked at me standing in my bottoms and no shirt.

Then his eyes darted past me to Zaria in a bathrobe and he tried to swing on me. I ducked and he fell forward like a dummy.

"Dominic what the hell are you doing here?" Zaria questioned with a flustered look on her face.

"Nah, the question is what the fuck are you doing here?" he inquired.

"Minding my fucking business!" she replied.

"You fucking this nigga!"

"That ain't your business! We are not together!" Zaria argued.

"The hell we ain't! We just fucked two nights ago, and now you out here fucking this random nigga!"

"Random! Nigga if anybody random, it's yo ass!" I retorted.

"Nah nigga, I been fucking this bitch since high school! You the random muthafucka!"

"Who the hell you calling a bitch?" Zaria asked angrily.

"If the fucking shoe fits!" he growled. "I can't believe you would do me like that!"

"I told you to move the hell on!" Zaria stated.

"You obviously have huh?" Dominic asked as he sneered at me. "I been calling your fucking phone! I shoulda known you was fucking some other nigga, but then I heard people talking about how the ambulance picked yo mom up last night. I waited to see if you would call and tell me what was going on..." He shook his head from side to side. "But of course, you were too damn busy!"

"Aye bro, you need to get the fuck out my room nigga!" I said. I had heard enough of this shit.

"Nigga put me out!" he dared.

"Aye man, you really don't want me to do that!" I stated with a chuckle.

"He sho' don't!" Zo said from behind us. "What the fuck going on in here?"

Once that nigga saw Zo and Rocky, all of a sudden, his whole demeanor changed. "Man, you can have that bitch!"

POW!

That was the second time he called Zaria a bitch, and it was going to be his last. I should've knocked his ass off his square the first time he said it, but they looked like they had unfinished business, and I didn't want to interrupt. But now, he had called her out her name a second time and that shit wasn't cool.

"Don't be calling my girl no bitch!" I warned.

"Yo girl huh? After I just told you she was on my dick two nights ago!" Dominic retorted.

"That was two nights ago. I bet she won't be on that muthafucka again!"

He nodded his head and rubbed his jaw. "You got it! You can have her!"

"I don't need you to give her to me, my nigga!" I responded as I pushed him towards the door.

"Stop touching me dawg!" he stated.

"Then get the fuck out my room!"

"I'm fucking going!" he fussed.

As he walked past Zo and Rocky, he seemed a little scared like he was worried somebody was going to sneak him. We didn't need to do no shit like that. We fought head on because we wanted the nigga to know what was coming. He finally walked out and I slammed the door behind him.

"Anybody wanna tell us what the fuck was going on?" Zo asked with a confused look on his face.

I looked at Zaria and she looked at me and we both responded, "Nope!"

The shit wasn't funny at all. I really felt some kind of way after the dude said she was on his dick two nights ago. We needed to have a conversation about that shit. I mean, we weren't in no relationship or nothing, but I thought we could have been heading there. Obviously, if she was bouncing on another nigga's dick a couple of nights ago, we weren't on the same page.

"Y'all good?" Zo asked.

"Yea, we straight!" I replied.

"Are you sure you're okay?" Jerrika asked her sister Zaria.

"Yea, I'm fine. He knew not to put his hands on me!" she replied.

"How did he even know you were here?" Saderia asked.

"I don't know. He must have tracked my location on my phone!" Zaria stated as she went to grab her phone off the counter in the bathroom.

She unlocked it and went to her settings I guess, to turn that shit off. She looked up at me with a puzzled expression on her face, probably because she saw that me and old boy had exchanged words when I answered her phone earlier. I didn't give a fuck about that shit!

"So, y'all good?" Saderia questioned. "Because I am starving!"

"Me too!" Jerrika expressed.

"We're good. Y'all can go on and eat," Zaria said as she continued to lock eyes with me.

"Okay cool. Holla at us if you need anything," Zo said before the four of them walked out the door, leaving me with Zaria.

"You wanna tell me why you answered my phone?" she asked as she stood there with her hand on her hip.

"You wanna tell me why you was riding that nigga dick two nights ago?" I countered.

"I don't owe you any explanation about what I was doing two nights ago! We aren't a couple then and we aren't one now!" she stated with her lips pinched together in a straight line.

"I thought we were heading in that direction," I replied.

"YOU thought that! I never said that!"

"You are absolutely right!" I admitted.

I walked past her and went to the bathroom. I turned the water on in the shower and stood in front of the mirror brushing my teeth. She stood behind me with her arms crossed over her chest and stared at me.

"What?" I asked as I looked at her in the mirror before I spit out the glob of toothpaste.

"That's it? You're just gonna hop in the shower?" she asked.

"Yea. You said what you had to say, so it is what it is."

After I rinsed my mouth, I took my bottoms off and stood in front of her butt naked. Her eyes roamed below my waist at my semi- hardened dick. I could tell that she was nervous, but I wasn't going to make the first move. I had done that earlier and look what happened.

I didn't say anything else as I turned my nude body towards the shower and stepped into it. As I began to lather the towel with soap, I could see her shadowy figure through the steam. She was still standing there in the same position.

"You ain't gotta stand in the door like that. I ain't trippin' and I'm glad I know where we stand now!" I remarked.

A couple of minutes later, she was gone from the doorway. I'd be lying if I said I wasn't disappointed in how things ended for us today. I thought I'd come here to Houston and show her some love and we'd go back to Atlanta as a happy couple, which was what I had been aiming for since we first started hanging together.

Obviously after what happened earlier, that was just something that I wanted. She wanted other things. If we weren't even on the same page, what the fuck were we doing? As I washed myself, I heard the door of the shower open.

I turned around and faced the girl who had just ruined all the plans I had for us. No words were spoken as she reached for my dick and began to stroke and massage it gently. The shit grew instantly as we stared into each other's eyes. With her other hand she reached up and pulled my face to hers.

She buried her tongue deep inside my mouth as she continued to stroke my dick with her small hand. As much as I wanted to push her away because of how betrayed I felt, the truth was that I wanted Zaria. She was my one weakness and as I pressed her back against the shower wall, I wrapped one hand around her neck and applied a slight pressure as I rammed two fingers in her pussy.

She hissed as she stared at me. "Fuck me!" she commanded.

And that was exactly what I did for the next thirty minutes or so. I fucked her long and good until the water started to turn cool. But I made sure that once we left this shower stall, she knew that she had a fucking decision to make. I tatted my name on that pussy up, down, sideways and any other position I could think of.

I wasn't sure where we stood by the time we stepped out of the shower, but I wasn't going to continue worrying about it right now. I came here to support her during her time of need, and that was what I was going to do. All that other shit would have to wait until we were back in ATL.

Chapter six

Jerrika

I was surprised when my sister said we were leaving the hospital. I thought we were going to just stay with mama until she was transferred upstairs to the rehab clinic, but that wasn't the case. She told me that Alonzo had brought someone who wanted to see me and they were waiting in the waiting room. After saying goodbye to mama, who was totally knocked out on pain killers and antibiotics, I followed my sister to the waiting room.

I had seen the guy around before, but we hadn't formally had the pleasure of meeting. "Rocky, this is my little sister, Jerrika. Jerrika this is Rocky."

I blushed hard because I was attracted to this boy... big time. He was about 5'10 with a light complexion and pretty hazel- colored eyes. He looked like a younger version of Jeremy Ray Meeks, the prisoner who went viral for his light skin and beautiful eyes. Rocky had locs in his head though and they weren't all over the place like some people. They were really neat and nice looking.

He was gorgeous and he definitely had all my attention. "Nice to meet you, beautiful," he said as he stuck his hand out to shake mine. I was so enthralled with him that I just stood there for a couple of minutes. "So, you gon just leave me hanging and not shake my hand?"

"Oh, I'm so sorry!" I said as I slipped my hand in his. The electric wave that flew through my arm made me think that I had been tased by him. "Nice to meet you too."

"Well, now that everyone has gotten acquainted, y'all ready to get out of here?" Alonzo asked.

"Where are we going?" I inquired.

"I thought y'all were hungry and wanted to take a shower or something," Alonzo offered.

"Hell yea!" Saderia agreed. "I sure do and I'm starving!"

"But what about mama?" I asked.

"Mama will be fine for a few hours! We can call to check on her every hour if you want to, unless you wanna stay," Saderia said.

I thought about staying with our mom because I was worried about her and didn't want anything to happen to her. But I was hungry and could use a shower too. So, I agreed to leave with my sister, Rocky and Alonzo. We walked out to the rental car and climbed in.

"What did y'all wanna eat?" Alonzo asked.

"Can we go by the apartment and pick up our things first?" Saderia asked.

"Yea, sure."

So, she guided him to our apartment where we grew up. I was so embarrassed to be here, but this was our old place. It was where we lived when we were in elementary school and did not define who we were now. The purpose of going to college and getting a degree was to make a better life for ourselves.

While we rushed inside to grab our things, Alonzo and Rocky stayed in the car to wait for us.

"Rocky is digging you," Saderia said as soon as we were in the bedroom collecting our things.

"I don't have time for that right now! Mom is in a crisis, so if he's here to make a love connection, he can forget it!" I snapped with my hand on my hip.

"Nobody said that's why he was here. I'm just saying that he likes you. Damn!"

"Sorry sis. I didn't mean to snap, but all this shit with mom and us having to go back to Atlanta by the end of the week is just too much!" I whined.

She walked over and wrapped her arms around me. "She'll be okay sis. As long as she sticks with the program."

"And we both know how much of a challenge that is going to be for her," I said.

"Well, maybe she will listen to the doctors and take their advice. C'mon, let's get our stuff before the guys leave us."

We packed up our things and Zaria's. "Where is Zaria?" I asked.

"Probably fucking Gotti!"

"No, seriously!" I stated.

"Oh, you thought I was clowning!"

"Really? She was just with Dominic."

"Yea, but you know that relationship ain't going nowhere!" Saderia expressed.

"I know. What I don't know is why she keeps messing with him if she doesn't want him," I said.

"I think she was just looking for some dick cuz she was horny."

"That's dumb though. Leave the man alone cuz all she's doing is messing with his emotions. That's never a good thing to do when it comes to a man... play with his feelings."

"What do you know?" Saderia asked.

"Just because I don't have a man doesn't mean I don't know stuff," I retorted.

Sure, I lacked experience with men because I only had a boyfriend here and there in high school, and I was still a virgin. Those two facts didn't make me stupid when it came to men and their feelings.

"Are you ready?"

"Yea." I followed her out of the apartment and locked the door behind me.

We walked the short distance to the car and the guys got out to help us. After they put the bags into the trunk of the car, Alonzo got behind the wheel and Rocky sat in the back seat next to me.

"You okay?" Rocky asked.

"Yea."

"Sorry to hear about your mom."

"Thanks." We sat quietly for the rest of the ride to the hotel. "I thought we were getting food. I'm hungry."

"We are. I just figured y'all wouldn't wanna be around a bunch of people since y'all just came from the hospital. I thought y'all might wanna freshen up and we could order room service," Alonzo explained.

I hadn't even thought about room service because I ain't never been to a hotel that offered it before. Shoot, I had never been to a hotel before period! As he parked the rental car in a parking spot at The Four Seasons Hotel, I took in the beautiful landscaping and nice tall building.

After the guys grabbed our bags from the trunk, we headed inside the hotel. The lobby was beautiful with its high ceilings and gorgeous chandeliers. We passed the front desk and headed to the elevator. Once we got to the sixth floor and exited the elevator, we could hear loud voices down the hall.

"That sounds like Gotti!" Alonzo said as he and Rocky took off running.

Sure enough, Gotti was in a heated argument with Dominic and Zaria was the topic of discussion as she stood there in a plush, white bathrobe. I knew this shit would come back to bite her in the ass. I just didn't think it would happen this soon. As me and Saderia rushed past the guys to check on Zaria, I heard a punch connect to Dominic's face.

"What the hell!" Saderia asked Zaria.

"Girl, I don't know. That nigga showed up here uninvited and shit..."

"How the hell did he know where you were?" I questioned. I mean, there were so many hotels in Houston. How did Dominic end up at this one?

"I don't know! I guess he used 'Find my Phone' or some shit! I know I didn't tell him where I was, that's for sure!" Zaria argued.

"This shit is crazy!" Saderia expressed.

Finally, they were able to get Dominic out of the room. I took Zaria's bag from Rocky and thanked him for bringing them up here. He smiled brightly and responded, "No problem."

I handed my sister her bag and asked, "Are you okay?"

"Yea, I'm good. I'm definitely gonna turn that app off now though," she said with a giggle.

"So not funny!" I frowned.

"Sis, relax! Everything worked out, right?" Zaria questioned, not taking the situation seriously. Maybe it was just me that couldn't see anything funny about it because I was already stressed about our mom and her medical issues.

"You ready to go?" Saderia asked me.

"Yea."

After we hugged our sister, Saderia looked at her and said, "Try to stay out of trouble."

"I wasn't trying to get in any. Trouble found me, not the other way around."

"Are you sleeping in this room tonight?" I asked Zaria.

"Hell yea! It's better than those damn hospital chairs we slept on last night," Zaria said.

"Okay."

I had nothing left to say. She seemed to have all the answers. I just hoped she knew what she was getting herself into. As the four of us left the room and headed to the one across the hall, I wondered if we were all going to stay in the same suite or if me and Saderia would be in this one and the guys in another one.

The suite had two bedrooms and a nice sized bathroom with a kitchenette and living room area, as well as an eating area by the window.

I was the shiest of the three of us. Saderia and Zaria were definitely extroverts who did not have problems making friends and shooting their shots, so to speak. Me, on the other hand, was a wallflower who had no problem remaining in the background.

People often wondered how me and my sisters were as close as we were considering our different personalities. The only thing I could say to that was because of how we grew up and the problems our mom had, we depended on each other a lot. When you only had each other, you had no choice but to be close. I loved my sisters more than anything else in the world, and I would ride with them no matter what. Even when I didn't agree with some of the choices they made.

Sometimes I wish that I had the same confidence that my sisters had, especially when it came to dating. I guess I had trouble talking to guys because I was so shy, but I didn't know how to break out of that. That was how I had been for as long as I could remember, and no one taught me how to be explosive and opinionated... not that my sisters were.

I just didn't think I could change who I was overnight. To be honest, I hadn't been trying to be anyone but who I was. I only had two boyfriends in life, and after dating a couple of months, they both friend zoned me. I didn't worry about it though because one just wanted to have sex and the other one had breath that smelled like ass.

The only reason I hadn't ended things with them first was because I didn't know how to break up with someone. I held no bad feelings towards either of them because I felt like they did me a favor.

Maybe I was too laid- back for them. Maybe they saw me as one of the guys. I knew it wasn't because I was ugly because I looked just like my sisters. Whatever the case was, maybe one day, someone would see me for who I really was and not who they wanted me to be. I wanted to take a shower, so I asked Saderia to order me a bacon cheeseburger without tomatoes or pickles and some fries with a vanilla milkshake.

She said she would, and I excused myself. I would have taken a bath in that nice ass tub, but I didn't want to hold the bathroom for too long. I was sure my sister wanted to take a shower too. I turned the water on and while it heated up, I brushed my teeth.

I had been wanting to do that all damn day. When I was done, I removed my clothes and put them in a grocery bag. Then I stepped into the nice shower and began to wash my body. After I was done rinsing off, I stepped out and dried off. I hoped the food was there when I exited the bathroom, but one thing I wanted to do was call and check on my mom.

As soon as I finished drying off, I got dressed and left the bathroom. "Where are we sleeping?" I asked no one in particular.

"You can take this room," Rocky told me. "I'll sleep on the sofa."

That was very sweet of him. Most guys would have assumed they were going to share a bed with me. I appreciated the gentleman side of Rocky.

I walked in the room to put my things away and called the hospital to check on my mom. Once I was transferred to nurse's station on her floor, I asked how she was doing.

"She's sleeping comfortably right now," the nurse said.

"Has she been giving any trouble?"

"No. She woke up a couple of times and complained about the pain, so we gave her some morphine and she went back to sleep."

"Is she eating?" I asked concerned since she was on a liquid diet due to the damage to her mouth.

"Not yet, but I ordered some broth and Jell-O for her dinner."

"Okay. Please call me or one of my sisters if there is any change, and let her know that we'll be back tomorrow," I said.

"Will do Miss Bacardi," she said as we ended the call.

After I hung the phone up, I joined everyone else in the living area. There was a knock on the door a couple of minutes later, and Alonzo went to open it. The waiter walked in with the cart on wheels. He pushed it to the center of the floor and left it. Alonzo handed him a tip and he walked out the room.

Once we figured out who ordered what, we all sat at the table to eat. I was really hungry because I hadn't eaten anything since last night and it was almost four o'clock in the afternoon. As I dug into my food, I didn't bother looking to see what anyone else was doing because I was worried about myself.

I looked out the window of this gorgeous hotel and thought about how far me and my sisters had come. Even though we hadn't rented this room, we were with people who could afford shit like this. Coming from the projects, as a little girl, my one dream was to get out. I had prayed for that day so hard that when it finally came, I didn't know how to act.

I mean, sure I wanted to leave home, but then it hit me that I was leaving my mama behind too. My sisters had no problems leaving, but I was the baby of the family, so I guess that was why it was harder for me to leave her. I almost changed my mind about moving to Atlanta and switching universities so I could be closer to her, but it was too late.

I had waited too long because too many accommodations had been made for my arrival. I had scheduled my classes, a dorm room was on hold for me... just too much was done. I just couldn't change my mind at the last minute. Mom wanted me to go. She said I would make her proud. What choice did I have?

I just never thought she would be in the condition she was in when we came back to visit. Now, we had to leave her laid up in the hospital to return to school. I knew I was going to be worried about her, but it is what it is.

After we finished eating, Saderia said she was going take a shower, and of course, Alonzo followed behind her. It still amazed me how my sister was in a relationship because when she first started college, I heard about how she was wild as hell!

Zaria told me how she was screwing everybody. I couldn't believe it. I could never just give my cookies to every damn body who wanted a bite, but to each her own. No matter what my sister did or didn't do, my love for her was unconditional and came without stipulations or judgments.

I was happy that she met Alonzo and that they loved each other as much as they did. I sat on the sofa and turned on the television. *The Adams*

Family was on, so I just left it there because I liked Wednesday. However, when I heard the moans and wails coming from the bathroom, I had to turn the volume up.

Rocky came and sat on the sofa next to me. He was trying to have a conversation, but I couldn't hear him over the TV, and I wasn't about to turn it down. He moved closer until he was almost in my lap. It was a little uncomfortable because I was nervous being this close to him, but it was the only way I could hear him.

"You got a boyfriend, Jerrika?" he asked.

"Nope, and I'm not looking for one."

"How about a special friend?"

"If you're looking for sex..."

He jumped up and held his hands out. "Whoa nah! Who said anything about sex?" he asked looking offended.

"You asked if you could be my special friend. I'm not stupid! I know how to read between the lines!" I responded.

"Well, if that's what you reading between these lines, you got it all wrong! I just meant..." He blew out an exasperated breath and said, "You know what? Never mind. Tell Zo I'll be back."

He stood up and grabbed a key off the table by the door and walked out. I sat there wondering what his problem was. Maybe I had misjudged him, but I wasn't trying to be anybody's friend with benefit or sneaky link, so he could forget that shit.

He better recognize!

Chapter seven

Ignatius 'Rocky' Cole

I had to admit that I only came out here to see about Jerrika and make sure she was good. I liked the girl and had liked her for a while now. But she was so guarded and shit. Like damn! Who the fuck said anything about sex?!

I just asked two questions and she practically bit my damn head off. I wasn't crazy to be looking for sex from her because Zo had already told me that she was a virgin. I wasn't out to take her cookies... at least not yet.

She was shy, but beautiful at the same time. Her innocence was what drew me to her in the first place. Most chicks in the ATL threw themselves at me because I had money and they knew I worked for Zo, but Jerrika wasn't like that. She wasn't impressed with my money, car or jewelry and I had a lot of that shit. My favorite jewelry piece was the one with my name on it and the little boxing gloves that hung from the letter 'C'.

My dad had given me that nickname when he realized that I could knock a nigga out with one punch. The crazy thing about that shit was I wasn't a big dude. I was only 5'11 and weighed 170 pounds, so I didn't look like the average threat to any nigga. But that was where they fucked up.

My grandfather used to always say, 'Never judge a book by its cover'. It took me a while to actually get what he was trying to say, but when I realized what he meant was that people's looks could be deceiving, I understood that shit clear as fuck!

Niggas thought because I looked like the average Joe that their lives weren't in any danger. How wrong they were! I knocked the first dude out when I was in the eleventh grade. I had no idea that I could do that shit at all. I thought that was a lucky punch, but when it happened again, I knew luck had nothing to do with it.

I had a gift, and after practically begging my mom, she finally let my dad enroll me in boxing classes at the gym. I had been doing that shit to pass time ever since.

I had been approached by a couple of people who wanted to manage me and turn my pastime into a career, but I didn't know if that was something I should do. That shit had been weighing heavy on my mind lately, especially since there was a boxing tournament coming up in a couple of months and the grand prize was a hundred G's.

I made good money with Zo, but this would be money that I would earn with my own two hands for myself. That was why I was trying to figure that shit out. When my dad brought it to my attention, I waved it off and told him that I didn't want to do that. Now, I was thinking maybe it wasn't a bad idea.

As I was sitting in the bar nursing a glass of Henny, this chick walked over with her friend.

"Hey, don't I know you from somewhere?" she asked with a smile.

Typical line that was good for both men and women. She didn't know me from anywhere, but she wanted to know me. She was cute and all, but I didn't come down to Houston for her. I came for Jerrika and wished she would open her eyes and see that shit.

"Nah, we ain't never met," I said.

"Aren't you from Atlanta though?" she asked.

"Yea," I replied as I looked her up and down.

"We work out at the same gym. You're a boxer, right?"

Shit, maybe she did recognize me.

"Not professionally, but yea."

"I've seen you at work and you could definitely be a professional," she complimented as her friend nodded her head in agreement.

"Thanks," I said as I took a swig of my drink.

"I'm Tamara and this is my friend Zoey."

"Rocky."

"Yea, I see it on your chain," she responded with a huge smile. "It's crazy how I've been wanting to talk to you, and it took for us to both be in Houston for me to finally get the nerve!"

"That is crazy," I said returning her smile.

"Me and Zoey were about to get a table for dinner. Would you like to join us?" Tamara asked.

"Thanks for the invitation, but I just ate."

"Oh okay. Well, it was nice talking to you Rocky. I'll see you around," she said.

"Yea, aight."

Her and her friend walked off and the bartender returned to fill my glass. "Man, those women were hot for you! Can't believe you just let them go like that," he commented.

"Already got enough woman problems," I said as I held up my glass to thank him.

"Yea, I understand that. But don't look like they would've given you any problems. Look like they were trying to hit you with a threesome!"

"What?!" I asked as I chuckled. "Bruh!"

"Nah man, I'm serious. I know the type."

"Well, I ain't interested."

"You gay?" he asked with a surprised look.

"Nigga do I look gay?!" I asked feeling offended.

"Nah, but who looks gay these days?"

"Well, I can assure you that I'm not!" I stated angrily as I swallowed the contents of the glass and left a twenty on the bar.

I slid off the stool and headed to the elevators. As I passed Tamara and Zoey's table, they waved at me with huge smiles on their faces. I waved back and kept it moving. The last thing I needed was a threesome with them two. But then again, with the way I was feeling right now, that might not be such a bad idea.

I stopped in the lobby while trying to decide if I should turn back and join them for dinner or keep going up to the room. After a couple minutes of thinking, I decided against it. I pressed the 'up' arrow on the panel and waited for the elevator. When it finally came to a stop, I stepped into the car.

I pressed the number six and leaned against the wall. Once it stopped on the sixth floor, I got off and headed towards the room. I hoped that Zo and his girl were done fucking so Jerrika could turn the fucking television down. I had been gone about an hour, so I was more they sure they were out of the shower.

I slid the key into the slot and opened the door. The television had been turned off and everyone was in their rooms. I decided now would be a good time to take a shower, so I grabbed some clean clothes from my bag and headed to the bathroom. After removing all my jewelry, I took off my clothes and turned the water on.

I stood and looked at myself in the mirror, admiring the nigga that stood before me. Before my grandfather passed last year, he told me how proud he was of the man that I had become. That meant everything to me.

I stood there flexing my muscles and admiring the toned biceps and abs. Then I stepped into the shower and lathered the washcloth with soap before washing my body with it. After rinsing off, I turned the water off and stepped out of the shower. I dried myself and wrapped the towel around my waist.

TAP! TAP! TAP!

I heard the soft knocking on the door. I went to open it and there stood Jerrika. She seemed like she had forgotten why she had knocked as she stared at me.

"You needed something?" I asked.

"Yea, to use the toilet," she said.

"Aight. Lemme step out then."

I brushed past her and exited the bathroom. She closed the door, and I stood alongside the wall while I waited for her to finish. Once she came out, I went back in and shut the door. I put deodorant and applied lotion all over my body. Then I brushed my teeth and got dressed.

I sprayed some cologne and put my jewelry back on before exiting the bathroom. I headed to the living room area since I had given my bedroom to Jerrika. I didn't mind sleeping on the sofa though. It was a pull- out anyway, so when I'd be ready for bed, I'd just pull the bed out and go to sleep. I sat on the sofa and turned the television on.

As I settled in to watch *F9*, one of the *Fast & Furious* movies, I heard a door open. I didn't turn to see who it was. I continued to focus straight ahead at the television. Jerrika rounded the corner and sat on the opposite end of the sofa. The room was thick with silence as we just sat there.

After a few more minutes of silence, I heard her take a deep breath. "Sorry about earlier," she said. "I shouldn't have come at you that way."

"No, you shouldn't have!" I responded, not looking at her.

"I know. That's why I'm apologizing."

"Apology accepted."

Silence filled the room for another ten minutes. "Zo said you're a boxer," she said.

"Yea. I like to box in my spare time," I admitted.

"Zo says you're good enough to be a professional, like Mayweather."

"Yea, I am."

"So, you ever thought about doing it professionally?" she asked.

"Yea. I'm actually thinking about signing up for the boxing tournament coming up."

"They have tournaments for that?" she inquired as she made herself comfortable on the sofa. She seemed really interested in what I had to say about boxing.

"Yea. I've never entered one before though. If I sign up, this would be my first time participating in something like that."

"What's stopping you from signing up?"

"I'm not sure."

"If you're as good as Zo says you are, I think you should do it," she encouraged.

"Really?"

"I mean, it's something you like to do, and you're good at it, so why not? It could be your big break if you ever wanted to do this professionally," Jerrika surmised.

"You sound like my dad," I said with a smile.

"Well, if your dad thinks you should do it, he might be right. Obviously, he feels you're good enough," she said with a shrug.

"You haven't even seen me box."

"I didn't even know you boxed!" She laughed. "Now I know why you wear that chain with the boxing gloves on it all the time. I just thought it had something to do with that old boxer movie *Rocky*!"

"That's actually where my grandfather got my nickname from," I admitted with a laugh.

"Now you have me curious about your skills," she said with a smile.

"I wouldn't mind showing you what I can do. I'm capable of knocking a nigga out with one punch."

"Nah uh!" she spat as she side eyed me.

"Seriously!" I proclaimed.

"You serious fa real!"

"Dead ass!"

"Wow! Alonzo never mentioned that."

"He probably didn't think you were interested. I mean, you have been giving a nigga the cold shoulder since we met," I explained.

"I'm not sure if you noticed, but I'm not as outgoing and outspoken as my sisters. I'm a little on the shy side and more reserved than they are."

"I get that, but you seem so guarded. I'm not sure if someone hurt you, but I need you to know that I'm not out to hurt you."

"Who said anyone hurt me?"

"I didn't. I said I'm not sure if someone did or didn't. I just know that isn't MY goal!" I assured her.

"What is your goal then Rocky?" Jerrika asked.

"To get to know you better. To spend time with you. Maybe to fall in love with you," I professed.

"Why me?"

"Why not you?"

She shrugged her shoulders and looked down at her feet. "You're a beautiful girl, Jerrika. You're smart and you always smell good as fuck! And you dress nice too. You'll break out of your shell when you're ready. Ain't nothing wrong with being shy."

"Thanks," she said as she blushed. "You're an alright guy, Rocky. Sorry I misjudged you."

"It's all good. At least you apologized."

"Well, I'm gonna turn in. I have an extra blanket and pillow in my room. I can bring it to you if you like," she offered.

"I can go get it, so you don't have to come back out here," I countered.

"Okay." She stood up and I did too.

I followed her to the bedroom, and she handed me the blanket and pillow. "Enjoy your night Jerrika."

"Thanks, you too Rocky."

I turned around and went back to the sofa. She shut her door and I opened the sofa bed and climbed in it. I laid my head on the pillow with my hands linked together behind my head. The television was still on, so I watched it until I fell asleep.

I was glad that me and Jerrika had cleared the air before we went to bed.

Chapter eight

Zaria

Gotti was one sexy ass nigga! He was the epitome of tall, dark and handsome. Because he was half black and half Dominican, his skin was a golden bronze color. His sleek dark hair was worn mostly in a ponytail, which looked great with his neatly trimmed goatee and light mustache. Those big, beautiful hazel green eyes captured everyone's attention when he spoke. He was six feet tall and weighed about 195 pounds, give or take.

I had always been attracted to Gotti but wasn't trying to get involved with him in that way because I knew he would hurt my feelings one day. I didn't want that anymore than I wanted to hurt Dominic's feelings earlier. I couldn't believe he had found me and showed up at the hotel.

Our relationship wasn't even that deep! I definitely would not have shown up anywhere he was just because we had sex two nights ago. He really gave me stalker vibes when he did that. And then he had the nerve to mention our little rendezvous! Who the fuck did shit like that? I didn't know niggas were messy like some females!

After I found out that he had answered my phone and exchanged words with Dominic, I was pissed! He had no right to invade my privacy that way. We weren't in any kind of relationship for him to do no type of shit like that! After he left me standing in the doorway to get in the shower, I felt my anger leave my body.

I wanted to have sex with that man. I removed my clothes and stepped into the shower. I wasn't sure if he would ignore me, but I hoped he wouldn't... and he didn't. That man immediately scooped me up and slid my pussy on that dick and took me all the way to heaven. By the time we stepped out of the shower, all thoughts of Dominic were gone from our minds, and once again, I was hungry.

"Can we order room service again?" I asked.

"You hungry?"

"Aren't you?"

"I guess I could eat," he admitted.

So, we put on our bathrobes, sat on the sofa and ordered room service. I wondered if me and Gotti should have another conversation about our relationship status, or lack thereof, just to make sure we were on the same page. The last thing I wanted was for us to get back to Atlanta and have him running around acting like we were together.

I decided I'd wait until the food arrived and that way, we could have a topic of conversation. Until the food arrived, we sat quietly watching television. Twenty minutes later, there was a knock on the door. He went to answer the door and the cart was wheeled into the room. The waiter waved goodbye and walked away.

Once we had made ourselves comfortable with our food before us, I broached the subject.

"Soooooo, I'm enjoying being with you," I started as he looked up at me.

He smiled while chewing his cheeseburger and said, "I've always enjoyed being with you, Zaria. Not just cuz we had sex."

"I know. I just wanna make sure we on the same page."

"Which is?"

"That we're just friends. I'm not looking to start nothing heavy..."

His facial expression clouded a little, but he recovered quickly. "We already discussed that," he replied. "I know you don't wanna be with me."

"It's not that I don't wanna be with you cuz I'm with you now."

"You ain't looking for a man. I understand."

"That doesn't mean we can't keep enjoying each other while we're here," I suggested.

"Yep."

I wondered if he was upset with me about that. I hoped not because Gotti had some good pipe and he laid it well. After dealing with my mom, I needed some of that to drain the stress from my body.

The following Saturday, we were all on a plane back to Atlanta. Mom's infection had gone away and she had checked into the rehab facility of the hospital. I was hopeful that she was finally making strides to get better, but I wasn't going to bank on it because she had let me down so many times before.

Once the plane landed, we got our bags and made our way outside where Alonzo had arranged for us to be picked up by a driver to take us to the condo he had rented for us. I was definitely excited about not returning to the dormitory. However, I wondered how the six of us and our bags was going to fit in this truck.

"Aight y'all," Gotti said as he gave Alonzo and Rocky brotherly hugs.

"You heading out?" Alonzo asked.

"Yea."

"So, you leaving?" I asked, confusion etched on my face and the lines in my forehead.

"Yea. Look, I'm glad y'all mom is feeling better. I hope she continues to move in a positive direction for her healing. I hope y'all enjoy your new spot because the area is dope! I think y'all will be very happy there. Zo, I'll holla at you later bro. Zaria, it's been fun. I'll see you around."

"Aight bro," Alonzo said as they did a head nod.

Then Gotti turned and walked away. I didn't know where he was going or who he was leaving with, but I definitely felt some kind of way. As we climbed in the truck and got comfortable, Saderia and Jerrika were talking excitedly about the new condo. I couldn't share in their excitement because my mind was elsewhere.

While they chatted, I just sat quietly staring out the window. I didn't know why I felt the way that I did about Gotti's departure, but I did. I just thought that he would chill with us for a bit. Him leaving us at the airport was totally unexpected.

"Sis are you okay?" Jerrika asked.

"Yea, yea! I'm good," I lied.

"Then why you're so quiet?" Saderia chimed in.

I just shrugged my shoulders because I didn't want to get into it while the guys were in the truck. I knew men gossiped just as much as women, so I didn't want them running back to tell Gotti I felt a way about him leaving.

The driver pulled up to the front of a really beautiful condominium with lush landscaping. My mouth hit the fucking floor. Even though I knew Alonzo had expensive taste, I didn't expect him to get us anything like this. I had no idea we would be living large like this.

"Okay, who lives here?" I asked with a huge smile on my face. "Cuz I know this ain't our spot!"

"Ssshhhiiiid! You better recognize!" Alonzo confirmed with a huge smile. "C'mon in and check it out!"

We filed out of the vehicle, and I wasn't surprised to see how cool Rocky and Jerrika were. The two of them had spent a lot of time together over the past week. I didn't think they had sex because I knew my sister was a virgin, but they had definitely grown closer.

Alonzo unlocked the door before he handed the keys to Saderia. My eyes immediately took in the high ceilings and the beautiful black wooden staircase and the exquisite wood floors. There was a huge crystal chandelier in the foyer and the crown molding added an extra level of sophistication to the spaces.

The first thing I noticed in the living room area was the beautiful fireplace and tray ceiling. The large island with quartz countertops and stainless- steel appliances in the kitchen were added bonuses.

"The good thing about this condo is that all three bedrooms have adjoining bathrooms, and they're all the same size. There's also a half bath down here for when you have guests," Alonzo explained.

"Who decorated this?" I asked.

"Why? You don't like my taste?" Saderia asked with a frown.

"No, the furniture is beautiful. I just knew Alonzo wasn't the one to pick all this stuff out!"

"Damn! I think I got good taste too," Alonzo said. "Also, all y'all stuff that y'all had packed up in boxes is in the closet under the stairs."

I walked over to the huge bay window in the dining room just staring out there. I wasn't sure what I was looking for, but I just felt sad that Gotti wasn't here.

"You okay?" Jerrika asked as she came up behind me.

"Yea, why wouldn't I be? Look around!" I responded trying to put on a happy face. "We actually live here now!"

"I know. It's so gorgeous!" Jerrika agreed. "Who woulda thought three lil girls from the Houston projects would be living in the lap of luxury?"

"Sure not me," I admitted.

"You wanna go check out the upstairs area?"

"Hell yea!" I enthused, but my mind wasn't really in it anymore.

I wanted to know where Gotti went and who he had left with. It was just crazy how we were just in bed together this morning and once we got to the airport, he had taken off with some bitch!

As me and Jerrika headed upstairs, I tried to concentrate on how beautiful this condo was. The upstairs was just as nice as downstairs. There was this huge bonus space at the top of the stairs and then a bedroom to the left and one to the right. After checking out both rooms, I decided to take the one on the right side.

Both bedrooms had huge king- sized platform beds with furniture to match. The room on the right side was a beige color and the room on the left side was like a blush pink tone. I thought that Jerrika would do better in the pink room since she was the baby.

Alonzo had definitely spent some coins decorating this place because he thought of everything. There were bath towels to match the colors of the bedroom and art on the walls. Tray ceilings in both bedrooms with a ceiling fan in the middle, and let's not forget about the French doors that led to the balconies. Up until today, I had no idea this area existed.

It was about a twenty- minute ride to campus, and since I didn't have a car, I guess I'd be using my sister's whip to get me and Jerrika to and from. Alonzo was definitely husband material to do all this for us on the strength of his relationship with Saderia.

After we checked out the bedrooms, we headed back downstairs. "Y'all hungry?" Alonzo asked. "We can go get some food somewhere."

"I'm kinda tired. I'm gonna go lie down..."

"What?! It's not even one o'clock!" Saderia commented as she looked at her watch.

"I was up late last night," I explained with a smirk.

"Do you want us to bring you something back?" Jerrika asked.

"If y'all don't mind."

"Well, get some rest," Saderia said as her and Jerrika hugged me on their way out the door.

I was a little disappointed in myself because as beautiful as this condo was and as excited as I was to get here, I couldn't believe I was letting Gotti get the best of me. I couldn't believe that he was occupying my mind this way when I should have been enjoying this lovely new area we were now a part of.

I decided to send him a text because I knew I wasn't going to feel better until I did.

Me: You busy?

He took about ten minutes before he responded and by that time, I was boiling mad! Like why the hell did it take him so long to text me back? What the hell was more important?

Gotti: Yea, kinda. What's up?

Me: I don't like the way we left things at the airport

Gotti: Wym? I thought we left things fine at the airport. I told you I was glad your mom was better, told you that I hoped she continued down a positive path and wished

you well. I don't understand what the problem is...

Me: Who picked you up?

Gotti: A friend

Me: A female?

Gotti: Maybe. What's with the third degree? You said you didn't wanna be tied down with a nigga, so that means we free to do what and who we want. I'm not understanding where all this is coming from...

Me: How can you be with another bitch right now after you woke up in the same bed with me this morning?

Gotti: Don't do that!

Me: Do what?

Gotti: Don't call her a bitch when you know that you didn't like it when that other nigga called you the same thing! You remember who I'm talking about right? The nigga whose dick you was on two nights before you climbed on mine! So, don't get mad at me for giving you exactly what you wanted. You said what you said, and repeated it to make sure you were clear, and I'm letting you know that I heard every word.

Me: So is this your idea of payback?

Gotti: LOL! Payback! For what? You didn't do me anything for me to have to pay you back for! I already told you that we were good...

Me: So we're good?

Gotti: Yea. I ain't got shit against you Zaria.

Why did I feel like shit right now? Why did I want him here with me instead of wherever he was now? He had basically told me that since I didn't want him, somebody else did. Normally, the shit would have gotten shrugged off, but we hadn't had sex before.

Now that we had, things felt different. I felt different. But I couldn't tell him that. I wasn't going to make it seem like I was begging this man to be with me.

Me: Thank you for the clarity.

Gotti: Actually, you were the one who gave me clarity. I wanted to be with you. I wanted to make you my girl. You made it very clear that you weren't interested in no relationship like that... at least not with me. Life is too short to sit around pining and whining over anybody, and I ain't about that life so...

Me: You're absolutely right! Enjoy yourself with your twenty!

Gotti: Hmmm! Idk wth that means, but OK! Take care Z!

Me: Yea, you too G!

I tossed my phone on the sofa and stood there with my arms across my chest mad as fuck! I couldn't believe I had allowed him to get me this upset. Why did I even care that he had run off with some other bitch? Why was that an issue for me at all?

He wanted a relationship, but I didn't... or did I?

"Dammit Zaria! Get it together!" I fussed as I picked up my phone and went upstairs.

There were plenty of guys I could be chilling with right now instead of whining over Gotti. But as I stared at myself in the mirror, I had to admit that he was the person I wanted to spend time with right now. I already missed his arms around me and his dick inside of me. I bet he was somewhere stuffing some other bitch's coochie with that pipe.

Now I was angry again because the fucking nerve of him! He didn't even have the decency to ride out with us from the airport and have that bitch pick him up from his place! What the hell kinda shit was that?

"Oh snap! Why didn't I think of that shit in the first place?"

I jumped in the shower real quick and then stepped out when I was done. I applied deodorant, lotion and perfume, Dolce & Gabbana Light Blue because Gotti said he loved the way it smelled. I threw on a light blue romper from Shein and a pair of white Vans sneakers. Then I made arrangements for an Uber to come get me since my sisters had left in her car. After waiting fifteen minutes, the driver finally pulled up to the front of the condo.

I grabbed my purse and headed out. I sat quietly as the driver headed to Gotti's place. If he had another bitch over there, I was going to blow a gasket because how dare he fuck me for a whole week then climb in bed with some other bitch!

He shouldn't need another bitch after the way I had put it down on him. I hope he didn't have someone else there, but if he did, at least I would know for sure where I stand.

Chapter nine

Jerrika

I was happy to be back in Atlanta, but I missed my mom. I was just glad that she chose to get admitted into the rehabilitation clinic. I knew it was what she needed to get better and if she hadn't done that, she would never change her ways.

When the truck stopped in front of the luxury condo, I was in awe. The outside was beautifully painted... cream colored with light brown trimming. The landscaped lawn was lush, and the flowers were bright and colorful. The property itself was new, so the trees were still pretty young. There was a two- car garage, but so far we only had one car.

As soon as we walked in, I couldn't help but take in the high ceilings and black staircase. I was highly impressed and could not believe this was where we would be living from now on.

"You like the spot?" Rocky asked.

"I love it!" I enthused.

"Yea, it's tight!"

As he and I chatted, I noticed my sister, Zaria, walk out of the room. She seemed to be distracted since we left the airport. I wondered what was going on with her, but I kind of had an idea.

Even though she didn't tell me why her mind was occupied, I had a feeling it had something to do with Gotti's sudden departure from the airport.

"I'll be right back," I told Rocky.

After talking to my sister, we went to check out the upstairs part of the condo. Then we made our way back downstairs and me, Saderia, Rocky and Alonzo went to get something to eat. Zaria stayed behind and I figured it was either because she didn't want to be a fifth wheel, or she had other plans that involved Gotti.

I had spent a lot of time with Rocky while we were in Houston, and I had misjudged him. I still was a little shy in his presence, but it wasn't like before we got to know each other. I couldn't say that I was ready to be involved with him in a relationship yet, but we could remain friends and see each other now that we were back in Atlanta.

Rocky was a nice guy, and even though I knew he was a drug runner for Alonzo, I still liked him. We laughed a lot because he was really funny.

We had just sat down at Old Lady Gang when I got a phone call from one of my clients. I excused myself to take the call.

"Hello."

"Please tell me you're back in ATL!" Katrina said.

"I just got back a little while ago. What's up?"

"Girl, I need my hair done before school starts Monday!"

"Aw damn!" I expressed.

"I already bought my hair!"

"What you trying to do?" I asked.

"A sew-in," she said.

"Whew chile!"

"Please Jerrika. I could have gotten it done by someone at the shop, but you're within my budget."

"Well, I can't do it today, but I can come by and do it for you tomorrow," I offered.

"Cool. What time?" she asked.

"The earlier the better, so I'll be at your room around 9:30."

"Great! I'll be waiting for you. Thanks for doing it on such short notice, Jerrika!"

"You're welcome," I said as I rolled my eyes.

We ended the call, and I went back to the table. "You good?" Rocky asked as Saderia and Alonzo looked at me while waiting for me to respond.

"I'm good. That was a client wanting to get her hair done today. I told her that I can't do it today, but I'd be there early in the morning to get it done," I explained.

"Damn! They couldn't wait for you to get back huh?" Saderia inquired.

"People were calling me all week, but I was in Houston," I said as I shrugged my shoulders.

"You missed out on some major dough!" Alonzo expressed.

"My mom means more to me than any amount of money," I said.

"I feel ya."

The four of us ordered, ate, got a plate of food for Zaria and then went back to the condo. "I'ma get a Uber to drop me back to my place," Rocky said.

"You want me to go drop you off in Saderia's whip? I gotta go by my place anyway," Alonzo said.

"Yea, that's cool. I didn't wanna put y'all out," Rocky stated.

"No problem."

"Bae gimme a chance to pack a bag real quick, and I'll be right back down!" Saderia said as she kissed him.

"I'ma hit you up later," Rocky told me.

"Okay. Bye y'all."

I slid out of the back seat and followed my sister inside. Once inside, she gave me a key to the condo. "Now that we're living here, are you gonna let us use your car to get to school?" I asked her.

"We will work things out. Don't worry," she said.

"But if you're sleeping over at Alonzo's house, how am I gonna get to campus tomorrow to do Katrina's hair?"

"You wanna come drop us and take the car back here?"

"If you don't mind."

"No, I don't. Just let me grab my things."

She darted off to her bedroom while I waited for her. When she was done, we headed back outside. Once we got back in the car, Alonzo and Rocky looked confused.

"What's going on?" Alonzo asked.

"Well, Jerrika has to go on campus tomorrow to do her client's hair, so she's gonna need a ride there. Since I'm gonna be spending the night with you, I'm gonna let her drop us off so she can take the car," Saderia explained.

"Y'all gonna need some more wheels now that y'all ain't on campus anymore," Alonzo said.

"We'll make it work," Saderia assured him.

He was quiet after that as he drove to Rocky's place first. Rocky lived twenty- five minutes south of where we did in a pretty nice area. I couldn't lie, but I thought Rocky was one of those guys who never left the hood... even though he could afford to.

"Nice area," I said.

"Yea, it is. I really love it around here," he said.

"How long you been living here?"

"Only a couple of months."

"Oh, so you're a newbie," I teased.

"Yep. Once I got the money I needed to get out the hood, I hightailed it outta there! Too much going on and too many people dying! I did not wanna stick around for that!" he explained.

"I get it. A lot of people don't get the opportunity to leave the hood unless it's to go to college, so I commend you for earning your way out. You should be proud of yourself," I said as I thought about my own situation.

If I hadn't gotten a scholarship to come to Clark Atlanta, I would probably still be living in the projects with my mom and going to college out there. But when my sisters decided to come to college out here, I decided to come with them. I loved my mom and missed her a lot, but I would have missed my sisters a whole lot more.

"I am!"

I had learned that Rocky had an older brother overseas in the military and both his parents had passed away when he was a freshman in high school. They had to move in with their grandparents and Rocky had a hard time dealing with the sudden loss of his parents. He couldn't concentrate in school and ended up quitting his sophomore year. His grandparents didn't agree with his choices, but had a hard time reeling him back in.

Rocky left their house when he turned seventeen and lived on the streets of the hood for a long time. He happened to meet Alonzo and apparently, he saw something in Rocky that he hadn't seen in himself. He and Gotti had taken Rocky under their wings, and I was glad that they did. I didn't know where he would be if he hadn't met the two of them.

During our long and late- night talks, we got to know each other. I was amazed by how much we had in common. Even though he was raised by two parents, they still lived in a house in the hood. We lived in the projects in the hood with our single mom. Our mom had an addiction that kept her from raising us properly, while his parents passed away in a car accident which kept them from seeing their kids reach adulthood.

I was sure that they hadn't imagined Rocky running and selling drugs for a living, but at least he was securing his future. I couldn't look down on him for what he did because he had to learn to survive on the streets alone. Of course, it was a life that he chose, but sometimes life was tough.

I was just glad that he made it through and had Gotti and Alonzo to look out for him. When Alonzo pulled in front of his condo, I was as impressed with where he lived as I was with ours.

When Alonzo pulled into the driveway, Rocky dapped up Alonzo.

"Thanks Zo, man! I appreciate you, bro!"

"No problem, bro. I'ma holla!" Alonzo said.

Rocky opened the door and stepped out and I exited the car too. I just wanted to share something with him in private. Once we stood not too far from the car, I looked into his eyes and smiled.

"I don't know if anyone has told you, but I am super proud of how far you've come. From the hood to this..." I stated as I pointed to his beautiful condo. "You did great Rocky!"

"Thanks, Jerrika. That means a lot," he said as he reached out to hug me.

I definitely allowed him to wrap his arms around me. This was the first time we had shared such an intimate moment. It felt good to be in his arms. After several minutes, we finally separated and smiled at one another.

"I'll hit you up later," he said.

"You do that."

I walked back to the car and got in the back seat as he waved goodbye. My sister turned to look at me with a huge smile on her face.

"What?!" I asked as I blushed.

"I thought you didn't want a man," she teased.

"Who said I did?"

"C'mon!" Alonzo said as he smiled at me in the rearview mirror. "You know you like him!"

"I do like him. I like him more than I did when I first met him," I admitted with a smile.

"I knew you would like him! That's why I brought him with me. I can see the two of you together," Alonzo said.

"Hold on now! We are just friends," I reminded them.

They were already convinced that we belonged together.

"Didn't anyone ever tell you that friends make the best lovers?" Saderia chimed in.

"We aren't lovers!" I laughed. "I do have a question though Alonzo."

"Shoot!"

"Rocky told me that he's single..."

"He is," he confirmed.

"Right, but does he have any female drama I should know about?" I inquired.

"If y'all are just friends, what does it matter?" my sister asked with raised eyebrows.

"It matters because I don't like arguing, and I refuse to argue about a man, especially a man that ain't mine!" I concluded.

"As far as I know, he doesn't have any female drama, and that includes baby mamas, exes, stalkers, nothing like that," Alonzo said.

"Good," I huffed as I breathed a sigh of relief.

"To be honest, I think you and Rocky would be perfect together because he doesn't like drama either," Alonzo stated. "Ssshhhhiiiit!"

"Who's that?" Saderia questioned as she pointed to the black Dodge Durango in the driveway.

"Some bitch who won't get the picture," Alonzo said as he rolled his eyes and drove the car in the garage. "She's the reason I wanna get an iron gate around my property."

"Is she your ex?" I asked.

"Yes! And she doesn't wanna believe that I've moved on," Alonzo said.

"Well, maybe she'll believe me if I tell her," Saderia said, ready for a confrontation.

"Nah! Let her be! I don't want you talking to her cuz she's always gonna try to talk shit about a nigga to get you to leave me."

He pulled into the driveway of the huge house and opened the garage.

"I'm not gonna leave you! And I'm not trying to cause any kind of drama, I just want the chick to know that we don't have any plans to break up any time soon, so whatever ideas she has in her head, she can get them out," Saderia stated.

Alonzo shut the garage door and told us to go in the house. "But I just came to drop y'all off," I said.

"Just give me a minute please," he replied. "Babe, just go in the house. I'll handle this really quick, and I'll be inside in a minute."

"Why can't I go out there with you?" Saderia questioned with her arms over her chest.

"Cuz this ain't got nothing to do with you!" The stern expression on his face let both of us know that this wasn't up for discussion.

Saderia didn't say anything else. She just turned around and went into the house, and I followed her.

"So, you're just gonna wait in here?"

"What do you want me to do Jerrika? Like he said, it has nothing to do with me."

I could tell that she was frustrated. He had treated us like children by sending us in the house. It almost felt like he was our parent and had sent us to our room for cutting up.

"Nothing, I guess. It's just crazy cuz here I was questioning him about Rocky having female drama and we pull up here and it's a female waiting on him!" I remarked as I shook my head.

I wasn't trying to get my sister riled up because I didn't like drama and confrontation and neither did she. If Zaria had been here, it would've been a totally different ball game because she didn't play that shit. Zaria was all about the drama!

While we were waiting for Alonzo to come back in the house, we heard yelling from outside. The woman was hollering for Saderia to come out. She looked at me with a questioning gaze.

"I'm about to go out there!" she stated.

"Alonzo said to wait in here," I said.

I wasn't trying to have no confrontation with that female. She looked wild as hell with that wild red hair, nose ring, and booty shorts.

"I don't give a damn! That disrespectful bitch is out there calling me outside! If I don't go, she gonna think I'm scared of her!"

"Why do you care what she thinks of you? You don't even know her!" I cried.

"TELL THAT BITCH COME OUT HERE!!" the female hollered.

Saderia didn't wait for me to say another word. She charged for the front door, opened it and went outside. I followed her because I wanted to make sure that she would be okay.

"I'm right here! Now what?" Saderia questioned.

"Bae, I told you to stay in the house!" Alonzo said as he ran over to my sister.

"Well, the bitch was calling me outside, so here I am!"

"BITCH!!" the female hollered. "You don't even know me to be calling me no bitch!"

"You don't know me either and I heard you call me a bitch multiple times from inside the house!" Saderia countered. "Why the hell are you here and what do you want with me?"

"I'm just trying to figure out what kind of relationship you have with Lonzo!"

"He just called me bae, and I was in his house! We pulled up in the car that he bought for me! What kind of relationship you think we're in?" my sister inquired.

I just stood there quietly as I studied everybody. Alonzo looked like a guilty man as he ran his hand down his face and rolled his eyes. The female looked like she had something to get off her chest and wasn't leaving until she did. And my sister looked like she was a hungry cat ready to pounce on its prey.

If she could see how her man was behaving, she would know that he was guilty as hell of whatever this woman was about to accuse him of. I had no idea what he did, but something told me that when everything came out, my sister was going to need my shoulder to cry on.

"Babe don't listen to her! She's just a hating ass bitch whose main goal is to break up what we have!"

"Oh wow!" the female said.

"Just go home Sina! I made my choice..."

"You sure weren't saying that last week when you were deep between my thighs!" Sina yelled with a smug expression on her face.

Saderia's facial expression changed from defending her man and turf to shock. As she turned her gaze in Alonzo's direction, I could tell that he was angry about what the woman had said.

"What?" she asked with her mouth hung open.

"That's right bitch! Where do you think he was when you called him to go run behind your ass? He was in my fucking bed eating my pussy!" She busted out laughing then asked, "How that cat taste? It tastes real good, don't it?"

"Sina you got two fucking minutes to get off my damn property before I hit up security and have you removed!" Alonzo threatened.

"Boy bye! I ain't scared of those damn rent-a- cops!" the female stated. "This bitch needs to know what a two- timing liar you are!"

Alonzo pulled his phone out and called for the female to be removed from his property. He stated that he had a trespasser and needed help immediately before he was forced to do something that would get him in trouble.

"Oh, you threatening me now Alonzo!" Sina continued to rant.

Saderia stood there glaring at Alonzo. He hung the phone up and approached her with a look of regret and shame on his face.

"Baby I'm sorry. I never meant to hurt you," Alonzo said.

The funny thing about that was the girl Sina was saying the exact same thing that he was saying at the same time. It was like it was a rehearsed script for a movie or something except she did it in a mocking and condescending tone. Me, Alonzo and Saderia directed our gazes to her.

"What?!" she asked. "Don't you think I've heard that shit before?! Lemme tell you something about Alonzo. He's very charming, extremely good in bed, and a master at manipulation! Don't be fooled by his suave demeanor and sexy swag cuz he's a liar above all!"

A police car pulled into the driveway and the girl's facial expression changed. "You called the cops!" Sina asked.

"I asked you to leave!" Alonzo argued.

"Nigga I can't believe you did that shit! And I don't know why when you gon be busting my door down within a week for this good cat!" she clowned.

"You wish!" he spat.

"Girl if you stay with him, you are a damn fool! Me and Lonzo been going through this shit for almost seven years! I done stuck around for this bitch and that bitch and I'll be around after you're gone too!" Sina stated as the officers approached.

"Seven years while he fucked other women! That makes you a damn fool!" Saderia shot back.

"Someone called for assistance," the police asked.

"I've asked this woman to leave my property several times, and she refuses," Alonzo explained.

"Do you wanna file charges?" the officer asked.

"I just want her off my property!" Alonzo claimed.

"Ma'am you heard him. He says he's asked you several times, so now that we're here, you have two options. You can leave on your own or we can arrest and take you down to the precinct to be booked and processed. Which do you prefer?" the officer inquired.

"I'll leave!" she stated angrily as she glared at us. "This ain't over Lonzo! It'll never be over, and you know it!"

She walked over to her car and got behind the wheel. The police looked at Alonzo and asked, "Are you sure you don't wanna press charges?"

"I just wanted her off my property," he said. "Thank y'all for coming so quickly."

"No problem. You folks enjoy the rest of your evening," the officer said as the two of them got back in the squad car and pulled off.

Saderia charged into the garage without another word. She went to get in the car, but Alonzo stood behind her and blocked her from opening the door.

"Get off me!" she argued as she tried to shake him off her back.

"Babe just come inside and let me talk to you for a bit. If you still wanna leave afterwards, I'll take you home. But I don't want us to end things this way," he said in a calm and smooth voice. "I love you."

"If you loved me, you wouldn't have cheated!" she cried.

"Just lemme explain cuz it ain't as simple as you making it out to be."

"I don't care! You cheated on me!" By this time, tears were streaming from her eyes. I wanted to say something but didn't think it was my place.

Alonzo wrapped his arms around her from behind and rested his face on her back. "Please babe, just have a conversation with me and if you still wanna leave, I'll go drop you home."

Saderia looked into my eyes, and I looked into hers. I could see that she was thinking about it, but I didn't think that was necessary. Alonzo had cheated on her and she had just been confronted by the woman. It was an open and shut case to me, and she should leave his ass. But what did I know?

I was single and had been for a while. I guess she loved him and what he provided for her, so maybe that was why the decision was so tough.

"Don't you love me?" Alonzo asked.

"You cheated!" she cried.

"Give me fifteen minutes to talk to you. That's all I'm asking for."

"Fine!" Saderia agreed as she shrugged him off her. "You got fifteen minutes."

"You want me to wait?" I asked.

"Nah, you can go," Alonzo answered.

"Don't speak for me!" Saderia barked. He raised his hands in surrender as she rolled her eyes. "You don't have to do that, sis. We already kept you here longer than we should have."

"I don't mind cuz nothing is more important than you!" I replied.

"I know and I love you for that, but I'll be okay. He has fifteen minutes to explain and then I'll have him drive me home," Saderia assured me.

"Or not!" Alonzo boasted confidently.

Saderia rolled her eyes and said, "Call or text when you make it home."

"Are you sure?" I asked, not wanting to leave her behind.

"Positive. I'll be okay."

"She sure will. I won't let nothing happen to your big sister," Alonzo stated with a huge smile like he hadn't just got exposed for cheating.

"Okay," I finally relented.

What else was I going to say? As they backed away from the driver's side door, I made my way over from the passenger side. I embraced my sister and said, "You call me if you need me to come get you!"

"I will," she assured me.

I rolled my eyes at Alonzo and got in the car. Up until what happened today, I really liked him for my sister. He seemed to be a really good man who wanted to provide for and take care of Saderia. Now, it seemed like he was no different from any other cheating asshole!

As soon as I got in the car, I hit Zaria up. I had to let her know what was going on, but she didn't answer. I guess she was tired and taking a nap. I couldn't wait to get home to let her know about all this drama. Only when I got home, she wasn't even here.

Chapter ten

Saderia

I was so happy to be back in Atlanta. Once we got off the plane, I was anxious to get to the condo that Alonzo had purchased for me and my sisters. They thought it was a rental, but in actuality the condo was purchased by my man for us but was in my name, just like my car. I wasn't nobody's fool, and often times, women accepted gifts from men only to realize that everything was in his name once the relationship was over.

I never wanted that to happen to me. I never wanted to be put in a position where a man got to tell me what to do just because something he purchased for me was in his name. I was way too smart for that. If me and Alonzo ever broke up, I would at least have my own car and home and a fat bank account to go with it.

But that was never going to happen because I loved him way too much. This man had done way more for me in the short time we've been dating than my own father had done in my entire life. I didn't even know who he was because me and my sisters had never met him. All we knew of our dad was that he was a white man with pretty green eyes.

My mom said he was married and lived with his wife and kids on the opposite side of town. That was good because if I ever ran into him, I'd have to tell him about himself. How could he have sex with my mom, get her pregnant three times, then dump her like a hot potato? Why the hell had our mom subjected herself to be with a man who was never going to walk away from the family he already had?

We didn't even know the man's name! It was like we had a ghost for a father and a drug addict for a mother. Well, that was exactly what it was! Now, mom had finally decided to get some help.

Thank God!

Once I saw how beautiful everything came together with all the furniture I picked out, I was thrilled. There were some things that Alonzo had also picked out that I didn't know about, but I was cool with the items because they added to the beauty of the place. I couldn't wait to get him alone so I could thank him in private.

Only when we got to his place, this female was waiting in his driveway. I immediately looked over at him for an explanation, but he just smiled and said he'd handle it. I had no doubt that he would, but he had a lot of explaining to do once he got inside. However, when the girl started calling me out my name and telling me to bring my ass outside, I did.

I wasn't no scared bitch, and I wanted to know what was going on between them. Nothing prepared me for what she said. I knew they had been together before we got together, but she said they slept together last weekend. I wanted to believe she was lying, but when she recited his lines of apology to me, I couldn't explain it.

I was so angry and ready to go home! After the police drove off, I couldn't get to the car fast enough. I was ready to get the fuck away from here and Alonzo!

But the way he held on to me and whispered that he loved me, had me wanting to hear his explanation. I could tell that my little sister was not happy with my decision, but she left anyway. Once me and Alonzo were inside the house, I sat on one of the dining room chairs with my arms over my chest waiting for him to speak.

He stood there looking at me for several minutes like the problem was going to fix itself. "You better say something or you can come drop me home!" I stated.

"Babe seriously! You gonna let an irrelevant bitch come between us!"

"She ain't that irrelevant if you were fucking her Monday!" I yelled. "I can't believe you did that!"

"Babe she doesn't mean shit to me!"

"If that's your explanation, you could've let me leave with my sister cuz this ain't it!" I griped as I stood up.

"Okay, okay! She doesn't live out here! She moved to South Carolina a couple of years ago for her job..."

"So! I don't give a fuck about that or where she lives!" I snapped.

"I'm just trying to explain what happened..."

"Then get to the fucking point!"

"She called and let me know she was in town and asked if I could drop by her hotel room. She said she needed my help with something..."

"Yea, I bet she did!" I scoffed.

"It's not even like that. I never intended to go there to have sex with her. I only went to help her out, and then I was gonna come back home. But when I got to the room, she opened the door without any clothes on! I'm sorry bae. I didn't mean for shit" to go down the way that they did, but I found it hard to walk away from her," he confessed with sad eyes. "I swear I ain't never cheated on you before that night!"

"And why the fuck should I believe you!"

"C'mon babe, I know you mad right now, but you know me! You know what kind of dude I am, and you know how much I love you!" he stated.

"You love me so much that you cheated on me Alonzo! Do you know how much that hurts?" I cried as my voice cracked. "I don't care what man walks up to me with his dick swinging, if we are in a relationship, I'm not gonna pay attention to his dick!"

"What do you want me to tell you? Women and men ain't the same bae!"

"Take me home please!"

"Bae really? You gon just run off and end things with me over some bitch!"

"Some bitch you fucked!" I cried as I punched him in the chest. "How could you?! I trusted you!"

"I said I was sorry bae!" he spoke as he tried to wrap his arms around me.

I shrugged my shoulders and tried to wiggle free of him, but he was stronger than me. He wrapped his arms around me and held me tight while I cried on his shoulder. I never thought that Alonzo would have cheated on me. I had been too good of a girlfriend to him for him to just risk it all for an ex!

He stroked my hair and back while whispering words of love to me. "I love you, Saderia. I wanna marry you, bae," he said.

That got my attention because we hadn't talked about marriage before. He had asked me to move in with him, but I didn't want to leave my sisters behind to fend for themselves. Marriage was a whole different ball game.

"Marry me?" I asked with a puzzled expression on my face.

"Yes! I've been thinking about our future. I wanna marry you and take care of you. I want you to have my kids, baby. You the only one I see as the mother of my children."

"We never talked about marriage."

"So, you never thought about the two of us tying the knot and you walking down the aisle in some fancy dress?" he asked as he side eyed me.

"To be honest, no. I mean, of course, I love you. I just didn't think that was something you wanted," I replied.

"Hell yea, it's something I want! You are what I want!" Alonzo said as he tilted my chin upward so I could look at him.

"I can't marry someone who's gonna cheat on me. I won't be sitting at home alone or with the kids while you're out there slanging dick!"

"I wouldn't ask you to marry me if that's what I had in mind," he said.

"Well, technically, you didn't ask."

"You're right. I just wanted you to know where my head was at. I know I fucked up bae, and I'm sorry, but I promise it won't ever happen again," he said.

I was so confused. I wanted to walk away from this man, but as he looked down at me with those pretty brown eyes, curly black hair, neatly trimmed facial hair, diamonds all across his top grills and in his ears, around his neck, on his fingers and wrist, I just wanted to kiss him. His sexy lips and that smile made me want to feel his lips somewhere else.

I pulled his face closer to mine and kissed him. He immediately opened his mouth and stuffed his tongue inside mine. He gripped my butt as the kiss grew more passionate and heated. He lifted my mini dress, exposing my bare ass cheeks because I wore a thong. He pushed me onto the dining room table and dropped to his knees.

He quickly removed my thong off and tossed it to the side. He wasted no time stuffing his heated tongue inside my honey pot. I pressed the palms of my hands on the table and braced myself for what was to come. One thing Alonzo knew how to do was eat pussy.

That man was a genius in oral pleasure. He pulled my butt closer to the edge of the table and licked me from the front to the back. I moaned loudly as his tongue caressed the center of my sugar walls. When he latched onto my clit and began to suck on it, I screamed with pleasure. Shortly after, my body began to shake profusely as my honey spilled onto his tongue.

"Oh my God!" I cried.

He stood up and removed his clothes before I could say anything else. By that time, I was laid back on the table as my body continued to shake. He stroked his dick for a few seconds before plunging it into me. With my legs in the crook of my arms, he began to pummel inside me.

"You love me?" he asked as he hovered over me while his dick slid in and out of me fast and hard.

"Yes!" I responded breathlessly.

"How much?"

"A... a..." He pressed his thick mushroom head against my G-spot and held it there. "Oh gawd!" I hollered.

"How much?" he repeated as he panted in my ear.

"A lot!"

He lifted me off the table and held me high in the air as he thrust upward inside me. I pressed my lips against his for a brief moment before I had to scream in pleasure as another orgasm erupted.

Then he sat on the dining room chair, and I stood up, turned around and sat on his dick. As I slid up and down his pipe, he wrapped his right arm around me and used his fingers to toy with my love button.

"Sssssss!" I hissed.

"Fuck that dick!" he coaxed.

I pressed my hands on his knees and began to buck on his dick like I was riding a horse. "Oh shit!" I cried as I felt another orgasm building.

"Yeeeeaaaaahhh! Fuck me baby!" Alonzo cheered.

As I rode harder, his thrusts matched my rhythm. Several minutes later, I released on his dick before he raised up and threw me forward on the table. He lifted my right leg onto the table and plunged into me from behind. By the time we were done, an hour and a half had passed, and we were exhausted.

We headed to the master bathroom and stepped into the shower. As the water rained down on us, I reveled in the feel of it on my hot body. All that lovemaking had me sweaty and spent. As Alonzo sat on the seat watching me, he smiled.

"You are so beautiful," he complimented. "You making my dick hard again."

"Stop it!" I blushed.

"You think I'm playing?" he asked as he stroked his manhood.

"I can't go no more right now. I just wanna finish taking my shower, and climb in bed," I admitted.

"So, you don't wanna gimme no more of that good good!" He pouted as he continued to stroke his dick.

"Do you know how worn out I am? You tore it up!" I admitted.

He stood up and reached for me. I playfully pushed him back. "Uh uh!" I teased. "Wash ya ass so we can get out of here!" I laughed as he nuzzled my neck.

The two of us finished bathing and rinsed off. Then we turned the water off and stepped out. After getting dry, we headed to the huge master bedroom and climbed in bed without any clothes on. As he pulled me close, he kissed the top of my head.

"I was serious when I said I want to marry you," he said. "I don't want you to think I said that shit just to keep you from being mad with me."

"Oh, I'm still mad with you."

"Babe, really!" he inquired. "After all that good loving I gave you!"

"After all that good loving I gave YOU!" I remarked. "Yes, I'm still mad! You still cheated on me!"

"I explained how that happened."

"Doesn't mean all is forgiven!"

"Babe, I can promise that it won't happen again," he promised. "I hated seeing you cry earlier, and the fact that you were crying because of some shit that I did... that shit hurt me! But I'ma make it up to you."

"You can't."

"Says who?"

"Says me!" he bolstered. "You'll see. Let's take a nap and we can go get something to eat when we wake up," Alonzo suggested.

"I have a question though," I said.

"Go for it."

"You said the chick lives in South Carolina, right?" I pondered.

"Yea, she does."

"So, why is she still out here in ATL?" I asked.

He took a couple of minutes before he responded, as if he were thinking about what I asked before he gave the wrong answer. "That's a good question," he finally replied.

"I know it is. That's why I asked!"

"The truth is I don't know."

"You gotta do better than that if you expect me to forgive you," I retorted as I rolled my eyes.

"Seriously babe. I don't know why she's still here cuz she does have a job out there and shit," he explained. "I'ma get somebody on it and figure this shit out though!"

"You would wanna cuz I ain't gon be doing too many more of those pop ups! That shit is embarrassing!" I expressed, thinking about the expression on Jerrika's face when I said I was staying with Alonzo.

She was my younger sister and looked up to me as a role model. What kind of example did I set for her today? I really wondered what she thought about her big sis now. It would literally crush me if I had tarnished her image of me because I always strived to be the best version of myself for my sisters.

I couldn't even blame the female for bringing her ass over here and confessing because that was her truth. She was a side bitch and tired of it, so she had decided to out my man on his deceptive ways. I wasn't going to say that all was forgiven with Alonzo because he had really hurt my feelings.

I had no idea he was having sex with some other female. That was the one thing I wouldn't tolerate in a relationship because my father was a cheater. He cheated on his wife with my mom for years. He had three beautiful daughters who he never bothered to get to know because he had a wife and kids already.

I wondered if he and his wife were still together. I wondered if my half siblings were older or younger than I was. I wondered if my dad ever thought about looking for us and contacting us. I wondered if he ever wished he had done things differently to give us a better life. I wondered a whole lot of shit, and maybe Alonzo was the perfect person to help me figure it all out.

"You said you wanna make this up to me, right?" I asked.

"Babe, I also said I wanted to take a nap..."

"Do you wanna make it up to me or not?!" I inquired in a sterner tone.

"I do."

"I need your help with something then."

"Anything," he responded in a groggy tone.

I needed to talk about this when he was awake. There was no way we could have such an important conversation if he was halfway asleep.

"We can talk about it when we wake up," I said as I snuggled closer to him.

He held me tight and whispered, "I love you."

"I love you too."

That was all it took for him to fall asleep. Within minutes, he was knocked the fuck out. That was when I remembered that I hadn't heard back from Jerrika. I was sure she had been texted me that she made it home, but I was busy with my man. I wanted to go get my phone from the front room, but Alonzo was holding me so tight, and he was so comfortable that I didn't want to wake him.

I would just have to wait until we woke up from our nap. I was a bit tired though because that dick wore me out. My mind was so busy with different thoughts that it took me a while to fall asleep, but I eventually did.

Chapter eleven
Gotti

Zaria had made shit crystal clear for me about where we stood, so on the plane ride, I texted my ex, Jordan to come scoop me up from the airport. Sure, I could've texted my little brother or someone else, but I wanted to get a rise out of Zaria. Me and Jordan had an on again, off again relationship for the past five years. That shit was tumultuous and she was a toxic female, so right now we were off, but she was my 'go to' girl when I needed shit.

I knew that I could always count on Jordan just like she knew she could always call on me. That was why I asked her to come get me instead of riding with Alonzo and the girls. I was sure that Zaria wanted her space since we had been sharing a room for the past five days and nights. The only time we were separated was when she and her sisters went to visit their mom at the hospital. Don't get me wrong... I wasn't complaining about that at all!

I enjoyed the time that we spent together. I thought it might have even brought us closer because by that last night, I absolutely knew that I wanted to be with Zaria. Since Jordan, she was the only other chick that held my attention to the point that I wanted to be in a committed relationship with her, but she didn't feel the same way. Knowing that she didn't want to be with me kind of hurt my feelings.

I knew I had strong feelings for her when she had me all in them. I never had a female tell me she just wanted to be friends before. That shit was new and made me feel like I was good enough to fuck but not to be her man.

When she sent the text message asking if I was with a female, I was shocked because she one, was the last person I expected to hear from and two, her line of questioning threw me off a little. I mean, if she didn't want me, why did it matter who I was with?

I smiled at that though because I didn't think my plan to spark jealousy in her had worked. She didn't seem too concerned about me at the airport, but I guess now that she had time to think about it, it bothered her. Responding to Zaria's texts started a whole bunch of shit with Jordan because she felt I was disrespecting her while lying in her bed.

"Who's that?" Jordan asked.

"Who's what?" I inquired, acting like I didn't know what she was talking about.

"Who are you texting?"

"Oh, nobody you need to worry about."

She turned on her side elbow on the bed with her fist propping her head up and glared at me. I rolled my eyes because I knew she was about to start some shit.

"The hell I don't! Did you forget where you are?" Jordan asked angrily as she used her hand to point out the obvious.

"Nah, I know exactly where I am," I replied.

"So, why are you texting another bitch then?"

"First of all, it's not that big of a deal..."

"It must be if I'm saying something about it!"

"Well, as usual, you're being overly dramatic. I'm responding to a message someone sent me first! It shouldn't matter if it's a female or a nigga cuz me and you ain't together!" I reminded her.

"Shit, we were sure together a few minutes ago when you were fucking me!" she snapped as she sat up with her arms across her chest.

"Did you hear what you said?" I asked as I looked over at her with an unbothered expression.

"What?"

"You said I fucked you! Not made love to you or had sex with you but fucked you! So, you know what's up between us. I don't get why my phone is any of your business," I replied.

"So, if I texted another dude from your bed, it wouldn't bother you?"

"You want me to be honest?"

"Damn right!" Jordan argued as she snaked her neck and smacked her lips with an attitude.

"I really wouldn't give a fuck! You wanna know why? Cuz the next nigga don't mean shit to me! But it sounds like you trying to start some shit, so you must want me to leave. And I have no problem doing that!" I informed her as I shrugged my shoulders.

She was quiet for a couple of seconds and then she responded, "Yea. You can take your phone and your text messages with that bitch and get the fuck out with your disrespectful ass!"

"Say less!" I smirked as I ordered an Uber before sliding out of the bed.

"You ain't gotta have an attitude," she said.

"You the one with the attitude?" I bent down and picked up my clothes and placed them on the bed then started to get dressed. "I was chillin'."

"So, that's it?" Jordan asked.

"What's it? You told me to get the fuck out, so that's what I'm doing," I remarked. "I mean, we done been down this road before. It ain't shit."

"I can't believe you! You asked ME to take time out of MY day to pick YOUR ASS up from the airport and I did!"

"And I appreciated it and thanked you for doing that," I said with a smile.

"You said you wanted to spend time with me and I was cool with that too! But now you mad cuz I feel some kinda way about you texting that bitch from my bed! That shit is just disrespectful!" Jordan fussed.

I shrugged my shoulders. "I done told you that I'm not mad. You got the right to feel how you wanna feel. She texted me and I responded. You said it's disrespectful, but I feel differently about it. I mean, it ain't like you're my girl and I'm lying here purposely being disrespectful. I think you keep forgetting that we ain't in a relationship. But I didn't see it from your point of view and now that I do, I'm finna go home. I'm tired arguing with females just cuz a nigga want a lil love! Maybe what I need is some time to myself."

"Just like a nigga to blame the woman for his ass being disrespectful! I don't know why I'm surprised cuz we've been having this same argument for years!" Jordan argued as she rolled her eyes.

"That's a lie! When we were together in a **"relationship"**, I never texted no female from your bed!" I argued.

"But you did from your bed while I was laying right there next to you!" She was quick to point out.

"Right, but from MY BED!! IN MY HOUSE!! I can do what the hell I wanna do in my own shit! The fuck!" I gave her a look that let her know I was confused about why she even brought that shit up.

Man, I was not trying to argue with Jordan right now. I came here for some fucking peace and relaxation, but she was trying to push me to the limit. I didn't know what the big deal was in the first place. It ain't like this was the first time I had done some shit like that.

"And another thing... if you wouldn't have wanted to have sex, we wouldn't have fucked! I was cool with just lying in bed with you and watching TV! You're the one who started stroking and sucking on my dick! Let's be clear about that!"

Her mouth flew open, but no words came out. Usually, she didn't give two shits if I responded to a text or not. If I had to take a guess about her sudden attitude, I would have to say that it was coming from a place of anger and jealousy. She was probably pissed about the week I just spent in Houston with Zaria, but I told her why I was out there.

Zaria was a friend, and her mom was going through some shit. I had told Jordan about Zaria when I first realized I had feelings for her. Why? Because she kept wanting to get back together, I wanted to be honest with her about that shit.

After I finished getting dressed, I grabbed my phone and my bag and headed to the door. "Damn! So, that's it huh?"

"What do you want from me, Jordan? You told me to leave, bro, so that's what I'm doing! It ain't a big deal to me! How you mad cuz I'm giving you what you want? What is the fucking problem?"

"Never mind! Do you boo!" she stated angrily as she waved me off.

"That's what I'm trying to do," I said. "I'ma holla at you."

Without waiting for her to respond, I walked out the door. A couple of minutes later, my driver pulled up. I got in the back seat and leaned my head against the headrest. These females were running me ragged, working my damn nerves and had given me the worse fucking headache!

Neither Jordan nor Zaria knew what the hell they wanted, and the last thing I wanted was to be caught in the middle of those two. The driver pulled up to my house half an hour later and there was Zaria banging on my door with an open hand like she was crazy. Did she not know that my doorbell worked? Because it did.

How the hell did she even get here?

"Looks like you got your hands full," the driver said as he nodded his head towards Zaria who was now standing on my doorstep with her arms over her chest.

As beautiful as she was, I wasn't in the mood for her shit. "You have no idea bruh," I replied as I exited the vehicle. I rolled my eyes as the driver drove off. "What are you doing here Zaria?"

"Where have you been Gotti?" she countered.

I didn't respond as I walked past her and to the front door. I unlocked it, shut off the alarm and dropped my bag in the foyer. She followed me and shut the door behind her. I turned around to face her and ran my hand down my face. What the hell was she doing here?

"Uh, I'm waiting for you to answer me," she said with an attitude.

"I don't owe you an answer, but you owe me one. What are you doing here?" I asked as I stared at her. She looked a bit uncomfortable as she swung her hair over her shoulders. "You were very clear that you didn't want me, which was why I went in a different direction at the airport earlier."

"Were you trying to make me mad or jealous? Cuz I know you left the airport with a woman!"

"I wasn't trying to do either cuz I don't play those type of games. I laid my feelings out there to you and have been doing that shit for months. I told you what I wanted from you, but it doesn't match with what you want from me. I want a relationship and you wanted some dick. Is that why you over here right now? You want some more dick!" I teased.

"Wow! Really Gotti!"

I just smirked and shrugged my shoulders.

"First of all, hell no, I don't want no dick! You probably just climbed out of some other bitch's pussy, so no thank you! You can keep it!"

"And you know that how? You didn't see me leave with anybody at the airport, and I caught an UBER here."

"I just know!" she insisted.

"So, what you doing here if you know that I was with another female?" I questioned.

"So, you're admitting it!"

"What if I am Zaria? Then what? You don't want this with me, and right now, I don't want it with you anymore!"

I couldn't help but notice the hurt expression on her face, but I wasn't about to let her fuck with my heart this way. She had me fucked up! As she stood in the foyer not saying anything, I waited to see what she was going to do. Without another word, she turned around and headed out the door.

I watched her as she walked outside and just stood there. She didn't have a car or an Uber waiting, so what the hell was she going to do out there in the heat? I saw her wiping her eyes and knew that she was crying. I felt bad and wanted to open the door and take her in my arms, but I didn't. I wasn't sure where this thing between us was headed, but if it was meant to be, it would be.

Right now, it just wasn't meant to be. I left her out there, picked up my bag and went to my bedroom. I went straight to the bathroom and turned the water on in the shower. After I finished using the toilet, I stepped into the huge shower. I was happy to be back in Atlanta and in my own home. If I had known Jordan was going to be trippin' the way she was, I would have caught an Uber from the airport and came straight home.

I lathered my entire body and face, then stood under the huge square shaped showerhead that hung from the top of the stall to rinse the soap off. I stayed in the shower for about twenty minutes and when I finally exited, I had never felt so clean. As I stood on the bath rug with the towel in hand, I began to dry off.

DING DONG! DING DONG!

I hadn't finished drying myself, but I grabbed my phone and pulled up the doorbell camera. I was a little shocked to see Zaria standing on my doorstep. As long as I had taken in the bathroom, I would've thought she had gone home. I did not feel like arguing with her anymore. I watched as she pressed the doorbell again with an attitude. I thought about saying something, but I just didn't want to deal with her anymore... at least not today.

She waited about two minutes, and when I didn't answer the door or respond through the doorbell, she turned around. A couple of seconds later, my phone began to ring. I knew it was her because her pretty face was the first thing that popped on my screen.

"Whaddup?" I answered.

"Why didn't you open the door?"

"What are you talking about?" I asked, pretending not to know what she was talking about.

"I know damn well you knew I was out here! I've been beating on the door and ringing your fucking doorbell like a crazy person for almost half an hour!"

"What you mean? I thought you left!"

"Did you see me leave?!"

"Why are you still here Zaria?" I asked.

"I don't know."

"Well, if you don't know, who's gonna know for you? Cuz you got me confused as fuck right now," I admitted as I ran my hand across my face.

"Can we talk... face- to- face?"

"I thought we said all we had to say, but I'll come let you in," I said as I made my way towards the door. I hung the phone up, unlocked the door, and opened it. I swung the door open and held it while waiting for her to walk into the house.

She stood there staring at me for a couple of seconds before she finally walked in. "Why you have to open the door in a damn towel?" she asked with a smirk.

"Cuz I just got out the damn shower!" I responded and shut the door. "What you want Zaria? Ain't you tired playing games?"

"You think that's what I'm doing?"

"What else are you doing? At this point, I feel like we going in circles. If you wanna fuck, just say that!"

"Did you fuck another female since you been back?" she asked as she stared at me while rocking from side to side.

"Why you wanna know that?"

"Cuz I do."

"You sure you wanna know?" I inquired.

"I asked didn't I?"

"Sometimes people ask shit, but don't really wanna know the truth."

"I wanna know. Did you?" she asked again.

"Yea, I did."

"Who was she?" Zaria asked.

"It doesn't matter cuz you don't know her. If that's all, I'm kinda tired."

"That's it?"

"What you mean? You asked a question and I answered... honestly. I ain't got shit to hide from you because we ain't involved like that. We just friends!" She stood there staring at me but not saying nothing. I quickly closed the space between us and looked down at her. "I know what you want." I grabbed her hand and placed it on my dick. "This dick!"

She tried to pull her hand back, but I held it there. "Grab it!" I told her. She tried to pull her hand away. "Grab it!" I repeated.

"After you was just giving it to somebody else, NO!"

"You knew that shit before you brought your ass over here, and you still came!" I said as I pushed her against the wall. "Tell me this Zaria... if all you want is a fuck buddy, why do you care who else I'm fucking?"

"Cuz I ain't trying to get no STD from you!" she barked as she tried to wiggle free of my grasp.

I held her in place though because I knew what she wanted. My hands roamed her body before I pressed my lips against hers. It took all of two seconds for me to drop my towel on the floor. As my dick pressed up against her, she moaned.

I quickly removed her clothes and dropped to my knees to orally please her. With her back pressed up against the wall, I drove my tongue into her moistened center. As I licked her pussy with my tongue, she moaned and hissed like a snake.

"Oh gawd!" she cried as her body shook over me. She placed her right leg on my shoulder as I sucked on her pearl. With my right hand, I toyed with her nipples on her breasts.

As her cream slithered down my throat, I quickly stood up, picked her up and pushed my dick inside her. She gasped in my ear while I drove my dick in and out of her. One thing about me... I had stamina. I could fuck for hours once I released that first nut, and Zaria knew that shit. That was what she wanted from me, so I was about to give it to her.

It was no secret how I felt about this chick, nor what I wanted from Zaria. I realized a long time ago that I had fallen in love with her, but I'd never admit it to her because this wasn't what she wanted. So until it was, I would keep that shit to myself.

But she could gladly get the dick though. Her pussy always clung to my dick like a new sock on a foot... snug. I loved that feeling and I knew that she did too. She wrapped her arms around my neck as I pushed deep inside her.

"This what you wanted?" I asked softly in her ear.

She didn't respond with words, but those moans and screams told me everything I needed to know. I went into the living room area and sat on the long part of the sectional sofa, so now she was on top. As I held her ass cheeks in my hand, I rested my lips on her right breasts. I teased her nipple with my tongue as she continued to moan.

She gyrated slowly onto my pole and cried out when I touched that tender spot deep inside her. I latched my lips on the side of her neck and started gently sucking. I ignored her light protests as I tattooed my mark on her. She may not be completely mine, but she was for now.

She finally managed to push me back on the sofa and as I laid back, she bounced on my dick. I could see the love in her eyes as she stared at me while biting down on her bottom lip, but I knew she wasn't ready to admit her true feelings. I had no idea why she was holding back, but she was.

After she released her orgasm, I flipped her over on her back so I could be more intimate with her. I long stroked her slow and steadily. She moaned softly every time I pressed against her G-spot. I wanted her to feel that shit in her heart.

Then I flipped her over for some doggy style action. I held her pussy open as I slammed into her over and over again. She screamed in pleasure even though she was trying to push me out of her. That shit was funny as hell too!

Ninety minutes later, we both lay on the area rug sweaty and breathless. It took everything in me not to express my true feelings to this girl. Those three words were on the tip of my tongue begging to be released, but I wasn't about to do it to myself. At the end of the day, I was a man and we didn't like to get our hearts broken.

Until or unless I got a sign from her about her true feelings for me, we would just continue this little game she wanted to play. After I was able to breathe, I stood up and reached for her hand to help her up. She grabbed my hand, and I pulled her up. As our bodies pressed together, I looked into her eyes.

She slowly pushed out of my arms. "Don't do that," she said softly.

"Do what?"

"Look at me like that."

"Like what?" I inquired.

"Like you wanna eat me or something," she whispered shyly.

"I did that already," I teased. "But I can do it again if you want me to."

"Uh uh! I gotta go back home and check on my lil sister," she declined.

"Your lil sister is twenty years old and can look out for herself."

"I know, but she's in a new place by herself."

"Why not just call her?" I suggested.

"Aren't you tired sharing your space with me? We were together for a whole week in Houston! I just need to go check on my sister," she said.

"Aight, cool."

I didn't get this girl. Seemed like every time we took two steps forward, we had to take ten steps back. If this was the game she wanted to continue to play, so be it. I watched her put her clothes on and even offered her a ride home. She smirked at me like I said something funny.

"What? I'm just offering to drive you home. I understand you have to go check on your sister, and I ain't trying to intrude on y'all time together. I'ma drop you off and that's it," I said as I raised my hands in the air.

"Okay."

"Gimme a minute to get dressed," I said.

I picked up the towel and went to my room to throw on some clothes. When I was done, I went back to the front and grabbed a set of keys off the hook near the garage door. She followed me out the door and closed it behind her.

We got in the car, and I opened the garage door before backing out. It didn't take but twenty minutes to get to her condo. I dropped her off and held myself back from leaning over and giving her a kiss. She didn't seem to mind though, so I just waved goodbye and pulled off.

On the way back home, I got a phone call from Jordan. I didn't bother answering because I wasn't trying to argue with her anymore today. Whatever she had to say was going to have to wait.

I decided to hit up Rocky for some advice since I knew Alonzo was busy with Saderia. "Hey bro, what's good?" Rocky answered.

"Bro, I need some advice," I said.

"What kind of advice?"

"Women advice."

"You wanna come over so we can drink and chop it up?" he offered.

"Sure, why not? I'm on my way."

"Cool. I'll order some wings and fries to go with the alcohol just in case you got something on your stomach. We don't need you fucked up if you gotta drive home," he explained.

"Thanks bro. I'll be there shortly," I said.

"Cool."

Half an hour later, I pulled up to his condo and parked in the driveway. I rang the doorbell, and he opened the door with a huge smile.

"C'mon in man," he said as he stepped aside. I walked in and headed to the kitchen.

"I thought you were the DoorDash delivery driver," he said. "He should be here any minute."

"Man, I just dropped Zaria at her place."

"What? How did you and Zaria end up together? I thought you left earlier with Jordan," Rocky surmised with a confused expression.

"I did. She picked me up at the airport."

"So, how did you end up with Zaria?" Then his mouth dropped, and he had a mischievous look on his face. "Y'all had a threesome!"

"Nigga no! That ain't it at all!" I denied. "What had happened was Zaria texted me while I was over at Jordan's place, so I texted her back." I shrugged my shoulders.

"And lemme guess. Jordan got mad!"

"Yea, bro! She threw me out and everything," I explained with a laugh.

"Damn!" he expressed and joined in the laughter.

"Right! So, as the Uber driver pulled up to my crib, guess who waiting outside," I finished with a smirk.

"Zaria!"

"Yep! Shocked the fuck outta me!"

DING DONG! DING DONG!

"That must be the food. Hold on to the rest of that story cuz that shit getting good!" Rocky clowned.

I had to either leave her alone for good or get her to admit that she loved me. The only way I was going to get Zaria to open up about her feelings for me was to stop making myself readily available to her. There was no way she showed up at my door earlier because she was worried about STDs. She was jealous because she knew that I was with someone else.

That bothered her... a lot! She wanted to play games and I was good at that shit, so let the games begin!

Chapter twelve

Zaria

Two weeks later...

I hadn't heard from Gotti since that day I showed up at his house and we had heated sex. I tried not to let it bother me, but I couldn't help it. Was he entertaining some other woman? Was it the same bitch who picked him up from the airport that day? I thought for sure he would have called or texted me by now.

I followed him on Instagram, so I was able to keep up with what he was doing. From what I gathered from his pics and videos, he had been busy. During that time, he bought a new vehicle, had been to the mall several times, and had even taken a trip to Columbia. Now that was for work because Alonzo and Rocky also went with him. I was not going to reach out to him first because I was the one who made the first move last time. If he was happy not seeing me, then that was just what it was.

It wasn't like I was sitting around pining over Gotti. School was now in session, and this was my senior year, so I had my studies to keep me busy. I didn't have time to wonder what Gotti was doing or who he was doing it with... but I would be lying if I said he hadn't crossed my mind a time or two. I hadn't had sex in two long weeks!

Gotti knew he had some good dick, and he knew how to use it. Of course, I missed it. And it wasn't like I could call Dominic to come give me some because he was all the way in Houston. And after the way we left things at the hotel, I knew he didn't want to see me.

Me and my sisters had been calling the rehab clinic to check on our mom every other day. We couldn't go visit her yet, but we were allowed to speak to her twice a week. The other time we called was to check on her with the nurses. Last time I spoke to her, she sounded a lot better than she did when we left her, which helped us breathe easier.

With everything I had going on out here, the last thing I wanted to worry about was my mom's health. Thank God she agreed to get some help!

As I sat at the kitchen counter doing my homework, my cell phone rang. It was my sister Saderia, so I picked up to answer immediately. I didn't know what was going on but all I could hear was her literally screaming through the phone.

"Can you stop hollering so I can understand what you're saying?" I asked.

"COME OUTSIDE!! COME OUTSIDE!!" she screamed excitedly. "BRING JERRIKA WITH YOU!!"

"Come outside for what?"

"You'll see when you get out here!"

"Jerrika!" I called out.

"What?"

"Saderia wants us to come meet her outside!"

She came bouncing down the stairs. "What for?" Jerrika asked.

"I don't know. She called hollering and screaming on the phone, so I couldn't understand her at all," I said as I shook my head. We walked towards the door wondering what the hell was wrong with our older sister.

Once we opened the door, we found out. She was standing beside a brand- new baby blue BMW sedan. My mouth dropped as she started screaming and jumping up and down.

"Isn't it beautiful?!" she asked.

"Uhm, whose car is this?" Jerrika asked, a look of skepticism on her face.

"DUH! It's mine!" Saderia yelled happily.

"Don't you already have a car?" I questioned.

"Yea! Alonzo bought this one for me so you guys can just keep using the Camry!"

"So, he bought you another car?" I asked.

"YES!!"

"A guilty gift," Jerrika surmised with a smirk.

"It's not a guilty gift," Saderia responded quickly. "Come on! Let me take y'all for a ride!"

"I was doing homework."

"Come on! I'll buy you something at the mall!" she promised.

That was all she had to say to begin with. "Lemme go put my shoes on," I said as I turned to run in the house.

I slipped my feet into my black Air Max 95 sneakers, grabbed my purse and locked the door. Jerrika was already in the car by the time I got back outside, so I climbed in the front passenger seat and strapped on my seatbelt. This was the way we usually rode around when the three of us went anywhere.

"Oh wow! This ride is fiyah!" I gushed.

"I know right!" Saderia beamed.

Ever since my sister found out that Alonzo had cheated on her, he had been doing a lot to get back on her good side. He had lost a lot of Jerrika's respect when she found out. It didn't bother me because my sister made the decision to forgive him and take him back. Also, I couldn't judge anything that he had done because I had issues of my own to deal with.

"Have you heard from Gotti?" Saderia asked.

"Nope, and I don't plan to."

"Why not?" Jerrika asked.

"Right! You know you like that man, so what's stopping you from reaching out to him first?" Saderia asked.

"I was the one who reached out last time! How come I always have to be the bigger person?"

"Maybe if you would tell him how you really feel," Saderia suggested.

"I'm not trying to go there with Gotti! Don't forget he fucked another bitch the same day we got back from Houston!" I argued.

"Well, what would you do if you wanted to be with someone who just wanted to use you for sex?" Saderia countered. "I'm not saying what he did wasn't low down but look at how you are treating that man! Gotti is a good dude and he really likes you, but if you keep playing these games with his heart, you're gonna lose him!"

"Oh please! He ain't going nowhere," I scoffed as I waved off her advice. "I bet if I picked up the phone and called him to come scoop me up right now, he'd pull up in twenty!"

"Uh huh," Jerrika said doubtfully in the back seat.

"What? Y'all don't believe me! Just watch!" I pulled my phone from my purse and dialed Gotti's number, putting it on speaker so they could hear. The phone rang until voicemail picked up.

Jerrika busted out laughing in the back seat and when I looked over at Saderia, she was giggling. "What's so funny?" I asked with an attitude. "He's probably in the shower!"

"You're right. He can't possibly be anywhere else but at home waiting for you to call him, right?" Jerrika teased.

"What do you know? Your lil ass not even in a relationship," I replied.

"Maybe not, but I could be if I wanted to and I bet if I call Rocky, he'll answer," she said smartly with a giggle.

"Do it then!" I dared as I turned to face her.

She pulled her phone out and dialed Rocky's number. She pressed the speaker and after the second ring, he answered.

"Hey you! I was just thinking about you," he said sounding like he was all in love and shit.

"Really?" Jerrika asked as she blushed.

"Yea, I was wondering if you wanted to hang later."

"Sure. I'm on my way to the mall with my sisters, but I can hit you up when I get back," she purred with a huge smile on her face.

"Bet! Y'all have fun at the mall," Rocky said.

"You already know. Talk to you soon."

"Aight."

She hung the phone up smiling harder than I had ever seen her do before. "Does Rocky know you're in love with him?" I asked.

"Girl what?!" Jerrika shouted.

"You heard me!"

"Sis don't play," Jerrika said as she blushed.

Saderia pulled into the parking lot of the mall and parked her new car. The three of us exited and walked towards the entrance. We always entered through the food court so we could grab something to eat on the way out the door.

"So, when are you gonna tell Rocky how you feel about him?" I asked Jerrika.

"When you tell Gotti how you really feel about him," she countered with a smirk.

"Good one, sis!" Saderia agreed as they gave each other a high five.

"I'm not telling Gotti nothing! I just call him when I need some of that good wood and then I come back home. No strings, no problems," I remarked smugly.

"But how do you know he's not getting it elsewhere when y'all not together?" Saderia asked.

"I don't know. As long as I don't see it, I guess we good," I explained.

"What if you do see it?" Jerrika asked.

"I better not see it!" I countered.

"Then maybe we should go the other way," Jerrika stated as her eyes scanned around nervously.

I finally looked in the direction her eyes were and saw Gotti walking hand in hand with some other female. "What the fuck!" I fumed.

"I guess now we know why he didn't answer the phone," Saderia surmised.

"Maybe we should just go," Jerrika said.

"Oh, hell no!" I cried as I walked quickly in their direction.

"Zaria! Zaria!" my sisters hollered behind me getting Gotti's attention. He looked up just in time to lock eyes with me.

By then, I was all up in his face. "What the fuck Gotti?" I asked. "Is this why you didn't answer my fucking phone call?!"

"What's up Zaria? Long time no see," he replied with a strained smile and nervous expression. He dropped the female's hand, but she just latched on to his arm.

"Who the fuck is this?" I questioned angrily.

If I had any questions about my feelings before, I certainly didn't have any now. The only thing I saw was red when I spotted Gotti. He looked like he would rather be anywhere but here.

"Who the fuck are you?" the girl asked with an attitude.

"Aht aht!" I snapped as I put my hand in her face. "I wasn't talking to you!"

"Girl if you don't get your hand out of my face!" she snapped.

"What you gonna do?" I asked as I snubbed her. "If you keep your nose out my fucking business, we ain't got no issues!" I snapped back before I turned to Gotti. "Who the fuck is this?"

"Gotti let's just go," she coaxed as she tried to pull him towards the opposite direction.

"What does it matter Zaria? I don't even know why you so mad! You already made your position very clear," he said as he tried to step around me.

"Nigga you better explain yourself!" I barked as I stood in front of him with my arms over my chest.

"I don't owe you no explanation!" he responded with an attitude. "As a matter of fact, I don't even owe you a conversation."

I nodded my head. "Okay, okay." He made a move to go around me again, and I snapped. I reached out and pushed him which caused him to lose his balance and fall backwards into the water fountain. Water splashed everywhere!

"WHAT THE FUCK Z!!" he hollered as he flapped around in the water.

"I TOLD YOU QUIT PLAYING WITH ME!" I hollered back.

"YOU THE ONE PLAYING FUCKING GAMES!! DON'T GET MAD AT ME CUZ I PLAY IT BETTER!!" he fussed as he tried to get out of the water. If I wasn't so upset, this shit would have been hilarious!

"Are you fucking crazy?!" the female asked as she shook her head from side to side.

"Shut the fuck up bitch!" I snapped as I snaked my neck. "I done told you this don't concern your ass!"

"The hell it don't! You pushed my man in the fucking fountain!" she cried. "Where the hell is security?!"

Saderia and Jerrika were laughing behind me, which only added fuel to the fire. Of course, that caused me to feel even more brazen than before.

"He ain't your man, but since you wanna defend him so badly, you can join his ass!" I yelled as I tossed her ass in the fountain as well.

She let out a loud screech as she flapped around in the water like a duck. "OH MY GOD!! OH MY GOD!!" she hollered.

"Uh uh, we gotta go!" Jerrika stated as her and Saderia grabbed my arms.

"I am not trying to go to jail behind this shit!" Saderia spoke with some humor in her tone.

The three of us took off running towards the food court. As we ran, I busted laughing at how many other people started running towards the exit as well. That was one thing about black folks...

when one started running, everybody started running. We made it to the car and got in.

Saderia backed out of the spot and sped out of the parking lot. "What the hell Zaria?!" she shrieked once she had merged onto the highway.

"What?" I asked in confusion.

"Please tell me you did not just push those people in that water fountain!" Saderia fussed.

"She sure did cuz I got it all on video!" Jerrika stated as she laughed from the back seat.

"I know you fucking lying!" I retorted.

"No, I'm not!" she replied. "I'll show you when we get home. Matter of fact..."

"I cannot believe you did that!" Saderia cried.

"Well, you were there," I replied smugly. My phone dinged and it showed I received a text from Jerrika. I opened it and there was a video of everything that had transpired in the mall, minus the first couple of seconds. "What made you record this?"

"Girl, I know you. As soon as you said aht aht, I knew it was about to go down!" Jerrika stated with a smirk. "Quick question though... why did you do that?"

"Cuz I felt like it!"

"But why? If you don't want him and someone else does..."

I turned to look at her because it sounded like she was taking his side.

"Don't look at me like that! I might not know much about relationships, but what I do know is that Gotti has been trying to get with you since before we got out of school for summer break. He came all the way to Houston to check on you when mama got hurt. Y'all spent the whole week in that room doing everything under the sun. And don't ask how I know cuz it was written all over y'all faces when we hung out together."

"I think what she's trying to say is you shouldn't be mad at him for turning to someone else when you made it clear that you don't want him," Saderia chimed in.

"Exactly!" Jerrika cosigned.

"Y'all don't understand!" I huffed.

"Then explain it to us sis! We're here for you, and no matter what we'll always have your back," Saderia said.

"Yep. Always," Jerrika agreed.

"I don't know what it is about him! It's like I want him, but I don't wanna get played!"

"What makes you think he's gonna play you?" Saderia asked.

"I don't know, but what happened between you and Alonzo keeps replaying in my head," I said.

"You weren't even there," she argued.

"But Jerrika told me all about it, and I could only imagine how you felt sis. I don't wanna experience that kind of pain cuz of no man."

"So, you just gonna keep playing games with him?" Jerrika asked.

"Shoot, after what just happened in the mall, he might not want shit to do with me no more!"

"I can't believe you shoved that girl in the water too!" Jerrika stated with a laugh. "And then she was wearing all white!"

"I bet it ain't all white no more!" I clowned. "But that's what she gets for sticking her nose in my damn business! I gave that bitch a warning! She should have listened!"

"What if she presses charges?" Jerrika asked.

"I hadn't even thought about that," I admitted. "I don't think Gotti would let her do that, and that hoe doesn't know my name!"

"That's crazy!" Saderia said as she shook her head from side to side.

"Love the new car though sis! Alonzo did a good job picking it out. So, does that mean he's all the way forgiven for cheating on you?" I asked as I side eyed her.

"Way to change the subject Zaria," Jerrika quipped.

"I'm just asking," I said with a shrug.

"We aren't back to a hundred percent yet, but we are making progress," Saderia said with a smile.

"Just don't let him buy your forgiveness," Jerrika shot.

"I'm not, but I love him. He said he wants to marry me, and he won't cheat on me again. I believe him when he says that."

"Just be careful."

"Alonzo learned his lesson the first time. He knows better than to fuck over me again," Saderia assured us.

She pulled into our driveway a short time later and we exited the vehicle. "Are you gonna apologize to Gotti?" Jerrika asked.

"What? Why?"

"Uh, cuz you threw him in a fountain of water in the middle of the mall!" she shrieked.

"Whose side are you on sis?" I asked.

"I'm always on your side, and you know that!" she defended herself. "You should never have to question that."

"I didn't until now," I said.

I understood where my little sister was coming from since she was always the peacemaker, but I needed her to just side with me and leave it at that. I didn't want her to question a decision that I made that I was already questioning myself about.

"Wow!" Jerrika gawked as she stood there staring at me. "I'm just gonna leave this alone before we both say something we don't mean. Your life, your business, so do what you want to."

We walked into the condo and I felt bad. I hated arguing with my sisters, and I hated it more when we argued about something silly. To me nothing was worth losing the closeness I had with them.

"Sorry sis," I apologized.

"It's cool."

She bounded up the stairs to her room.

"She'll be fine, but she was right about one thing... you do owe Gotti an apology," Saderia said.

"Well, whether I owe him one or not, he ain't getting it, so let's drop it. I don't wanna argue with you too," I said. "You didn't park in the garage. Are you leaving?"

"Yea, me and Alonzo are going out to dinner."

"Must be nice," I remarked.

"It is. If you gave Gotti a chance, you might be enjoying the same treatment," Saderia stated with a smirk.

"Whatever!"

She disappeared in her room and a short time later, the doorbell rang. I opened the door without looking to see who it was first and there was Gotti, soaking wet.

He brushed past me angrily and asked, "What the fuck is wrong with you Zaria?!"

"What?" I asked innocently as I shut the door.

"What the fuck you mean what?! Look at me!" he fussed as he held his hands out.

Trying to hold in my laughter, I shrugged my shoulders. "You deserved that shit!"

"The fuck! You had no right to do me and that girl like that!"

"The hell I didn't! You disrespected me!"

"HOW SO?!! HOW THE FUCK DID I DO THAT?!!" he questioned as he glared at me.

"You know exactly how you did it and stop cussing me in my house!" I retorted.

"I don't know what you want from me Zaria! I don't even think you know what the fuck you want, but I'm sick and tired of playing these damn games with you! You told me you didn't wanna be with me, so fuck it, I moved on!"

"Oh, is that what you did? You moved on with that cheap dollar store Barbie knock- off!"

"What does it matter if you don't want me?!" he questioned. "I ain't seen or heard from you in two weeks!"

"The phone works both ways!" I countered.

"Look Zaria, I don't know what your angle is or why you keep playing with my nerves like that, but I ain't got time for that shit!"

I had never seen this side of Gotti. He was sexy as fuck and the way he was talking to me had me feeling real horny. But the look on his face told me that now was not the time to try and seduce him.

"I ain't playing games!" I argued.

"That's all you've done since we met! You want the dick but not the man, which doesn't make sense cuz me and my dick are a package deal!"

"Boy ain't nobody worrying about your dick!" I scoffed.

"You and I both know you lying!" Gotti teased. "But if that's how you wanna play it, fine! Just don't get mad when you see me around the city with another chick!"

"Stop disrespecting me!" I fussed.

"Grow the hell up Zaria!" Gotti argued.

That shit stung more than he probably intended it to. I wanted to slap him because I felt like he was criticizing me, but considering how pissed he was, I kept my hands to myself.

"I am grown!" I retorted.

"I can't tell! You acted like a fucking kid in that mall! I tried to keep the shit civilized..."

"Civilized my ass! And I am grown! Take a good look," I said as I twirled for him to see.

"What I see is a little girl scared to fall in love, and instead of keeping it real with a nigga, you wanna play all these games with me. The shit was cute in the beginning, but it ain't no more! It's childish and pathetic!" he blared angrily.

I opened my mouth to say something, but nothing would come out. Saderia finally entered the room and asked, "Is everything alright?"

"Yea, we good. Do me a favor. Next time you with your sister and y'all happen to see me, turn the other way cuz this the first and only time she gon get away with that shit she pulled today!" Gotti sneered. He turned to leave, and I heard him mumbling on his way out. "Had me walking around that fucking mall looking like a damn fool!"

He opened the door and walked out. "You just gon let him leave?" Saderia asked.

"What the hell you want me to do? He just called me childish!"

"Well, you were a bit childish sis!"

"Not you too!"

"I'm just saying. You owe him an apology," she said.

"He'll be alright. I'ma text or call him in a couple of days for some dick and everything gon be fine," I said with a laugh.

"See... that's childish. He's in the driveway and instead of going out there and apologizing, you gonna let a couple of days go by then call him for some dick!" Saderia fussed as she shook her head. "You're gonna lose him."

"If I lose him, it's cuz we weren't meant to be in the first place, not because of anything I did or didn't do," I surmised with a shrug of my shoulders.

"Well, I'll see y'all later in the week," Saderia said as she embraced me before heading out the door.

"Okay. Enjoy your dinner."

"I will."

She walked out the door and locked it behind her. I flopped down on the sofa and stared up at the ceiling. Maybe I had gone a little far with Gotti considering how upset he was, but it wasn't my fault. When I saw him walking with that bitch, holding hands and laughing, I just lost it. I didn't want to see him with no other female.

I had no clue that I was keeping in feelings like that for Gotti. I knew I cared about him a lot more than I was willing to admit. If I had known he was in the mall with some female, I never would have gone because I didn't want to see that! My blood started boiling as soon as I saw them together.

I couldn't have stopped myself from reacting even if I wanted to. I had no intentions on pushing them in that fountain water though. That jus happened.

"What to do... what to do!" I expressed as I blew out a breath.

I needed to figure out what I wanted as far as Gotti was concerned because the aggravation in his tone earlier let me know that he was done with my little charade. If I had to be honest with myself, I'd have to admit that I missed Gotti over the past two weeks. I didn't know what I was going to do.

Chapter thirteen

Saderia

A month later...

Things between me and Alonzo had been going really well since we made up. He had done everything possible to let me know how much he loved me. When he said he wouldn't cheat on me again, I believed him. It was a little hard for me to fully trust him the way that I did before, but since I wanted our relationship to work, I put my trust in him and tried to put that mess behind us.

Over the past month, I barely spent any time at the new condo. I spent most of my time at Alonzo's house. "I told you that you need to move in," he said from behind me.

"I know."

"I mean, how many nights have you spent at the condo?" he questioned.

"I don't know."

"Two!" he answered as he held up two fingers. "Why are you having a hard time making the decision to move here? And don't say because of your sisters. They've been taking care of themselves the past few weeks."

"You're right."

"So, what's the problem?"

"There is no problem," I said.

"You know I'm gonna marry you, right? So, once we jump that broom, you won't have a choice but to move in. Might as well do it now and get it over with," he reasoned.

Even though he had been saying he was going to marry me, he had yet to propose to me. I wasn't trying to push him into doing something he wasn't ready to do but having that extra incentive would make things easier.

"Okay."

"Did you say okay?" he asked with a huge smile on his handsome face.

"I said okay."

He scooped me up and twirled me around. I screamed excitedly as he put me down. "I'm glad you finally said yes!"

"I can tell."

"So, when are you gonna tell your sisters and go get your things?"

"Slow down babe. I just agreed," I said with a chuckle.

"I know, but I'm excited. I ain't never asked nobody to move in here with me before," he said.

"Really!"

"Yea. I don't be asking just anybody."

"Well, that's good to know."

Me and Alonzo were talking about the next step in our relationship when I got a phone call from the hospital. "Hello," I answered.

"Yes, is this Saderia Bacardi?"

"Yes, it is."

"Miss Bacardi, my name is Cordelia Sparks. I'm a nurse at the rehab clinic where your mother was being housed for treatment," she explained, which immediately put me on edge.

"Is my mom okay?" I asked nervously.

"I'm not sure how to tell you this but she signed herself out of the clinic," she informed me.

"What?! When?!"

"Three days ago."

"Why are you just now calling me?" I asked hysterically.

"I apologize for you not getting informed sooner. We aren't obligated to contact the family unless something happens to their loved ones. Because your mom is an adult, she is allowed to sign herself out because she signed herself in for treatment voluntarily," the nurse explained.

"Wooow! So, you have no idea where she is!"

"No ma'am. If she happens to come back..."

"She's not coming back! She didn't even wanna stay in the first place!" I argued. "For all we know, she could be strung out on drugs again somewhere!"

"Again, I'm sorry."

"Yea, thanks for calling." I hung the phone up and looked at Alonzo. "Our mom signed herself out of rehab!"

"Damn!"

"I don't even know how to reach her!" I cried.

"Maybe she's okay. Maybe she's cured. Try calling her cell phone," he suggested.

"She sold it!"

"Aw damn! What about a house phone at your old place?"

"I don't even know if it's still in service," I said as I dialed the house phone. The operator came on saying that the line was disconnected. I hung up and looked at Alonzo again. "It's disconnected!"

"Damn! Okay, lemme see if I can get one of my buddies in H-Town to go ride by her place to check on her," Alonzo said.

He pulled out his phone but before he was able to call anyone, the doorbell rang. While he went to see who was at the door, I called my sisters to let them know the latest news about mom. Before they answered, I heard commotion at the front door.

I jumped up when I heard a female's voice. "Babe, what's going on?" I asked.

The woman he had slept with was at the front door. "Why is she here?" Sina asked with a grimace.

"I live here!" I pointed out. "Why are you here?"

"You moved her in your house Zo! Really!"

"Yes. What can I do for you Sina?" Alonzo asked.

"Well, since you moving bitches in and shit, how about getting a room ready for your baby mama?!" she asked as she rubbed her small belly.

"The fuck!" Alonzo stated in shock.

"Oh hell naw!" I remarked.

"Oh, hell yes!" Sina rejoiced with a huge smile. "This situation might be a little uncomfortable, but I'm willing to try and make it work." She busted out laughing as she walked into the house.

I looked at Alonzo with my mouth hung open. Tears threatened to fall from my eyes. This was just too much...

To be continued...

Made in the USA
Monee, IL
03 October 2023

43894638R10142